STORM AT ARBERTH

To my daughter, my daughter-in-law and my three sons

STORM AT ARBERTH

SIÂN JAMES

seren

seren is the imprint of
Poetry Wales Press Ltd
Wyndham Street, Bridgend
Mid Glamorgan, Wales

A British Library Cataloguing in Publication Record
is available at the CIP Office

ISBN 1-85411-111-6

Cover illustration:
'Waiting for the Moment' by Alan Salisbury
(Monoprint collage pen and ink)

*The publisher acknowledges the financial support of the
Arts Council of Wales*

Printed in Palatino by WBC Bookbinders, Bridgend

STORM AT ARBERTH

ONE

I t's a lovely cottage,' Sally said, in what Marian always thought of as her tragedy voice. 'It's quaint. It seems strange that I've never been here before.'

'You've been asked often enough,' Marian said. 'You and Alan went abroad every summer.'

She bustled about trying not to notice Sally's tears. Sally's moods had always unnerved her. 'Do sit down. Or do you want to take your things upstairs? Shall I show you the bathroom and your bedroom?'

But Sally neither sat down nor seemed ready to be taken upstairs. She stood at the small sitting-room window and stared out at the green valley, saying not a word. After a minute or so she laid her forehead on the glass.

Marian had forgotten how badly-behaved Sally was. She'd remembered the occasional sulks and tantrums, but not the rudeness. One shouldn't, she said to herself, have to make allowances for a woman of her age.

'You must be tired,' she said then. 'Will you have a sherry?'

'Do you have gin?'

'I'm afraid not. I don't buy anything but sherry and whisky. And lager when the boys are home.'

'I'll have whisky.'

'Please,' Marian said to herself.

'I'll have to buy another bottle tomorrow,' she said aloud. 'This is almost empty. You'll find me a pretty poor hostess, I haven't had anyone but the boys' friends here for two or three years. I don't even have many callers nowadays.'

Sally took off her silk jacket and sat down. She seemed a little more composed, Marian thought, with a glass in her hand. All the same, she wished she hadn't invited her to stay. Or had she had any choice? Probably not.

She poured herself a sherry.

'I haven't had time to make much of a meal,' she said. 'I've got some gammon steaks.'

'That'll be fine. I never notice what I'm eating these days. Do you mind if I smoke?'

'Well...' Marian started to say, but decided it was easier to fetch an ash-tray.

How am I going to cope, she asked herself as she sipped her sherry. She's so self-indulgent — just as she was at college. Only then it seemed more excusable. How is it that she hasn't changed at all? She should have learnt some restraint, acquired some maturity.

'Shall I top you up?' she asked. And then, 'How's Virginia? I haven't seen her for years. Is she still as pretty?'

Sally turned towards her and held out her glass.

The silence in the room seemed to tremble as Marian waited for an answer.

'She's pretty enough,' Sally said at last in her deepest voice and her most off-hand manner. 'She's well enough too, I suppose. But she's living with such an awful man.'

Sally's voice was famous. Marian suddenly remembered how she used to practise saying 'You rotter,' for some play at college. 'You rotter. I'll never forgive you.' It was a terrible play.

She clicked her sympathy. 'But would we have thought him awful when we were in college?' she asked after another silence. 'Do you remember that dreadful commercial traveller you used to go out with? One night I hid your best shoes to stop you going to meet him. I was sure he was married. Apart from everything else.'

'I don't remember any commercial traveller,' Sally said.

'Of course you do. He used to bring you samples. Yardley soap and Tampax and Vaseline shampoo.'

How could she pretend not to remember? 'I'll get the supper,' she said, sighing a little.

It wasn't as though Sally appreciated her husband when she had him, she told herself in the kitchen. She was always gallivanting about with other men. The last time we met she had someone in tow. Felix Somebody; said they'd met by accident in the Tube and did I mind if he joined us for dinner. They didn't behave like people who'd happened to run into each other in the Tube. Why do I put up with her? She's always on about how close we were at college and I'm foolish enough to go along with it. We were only close because we shared a room. And that not by design — not in the first year. In the second and third years, yes, though why I can't imagine.

Her mood changed abruptly. I was proud to be her friend, that's why. She was special, that's why. There wasn't anyone like her, that's why.

She went back to the sitting-room engulfed by a wave of affection towards her. 'It's lovely to have you here,' she said.

Sally turned from the window and looked up at her. 'My life is over,' she said.

Marian rushed to her side and put her arms round her. 'I thought that when Dickie died,' she whispered. 'But now I'm happy again.'

'Oh Marian, I feel torn apart. When he asked me for a divorce I thought he was joking. I thought he was getting at me because I'd been out such a lot. It was our Christmas panto, I was directing it — as well as being Principal Boy, I mean — I *had* to be out a lot, almost every night. "We'll go away together when it's over," I said. "Shall we? A long weekend at that beach hotel in Devon. It'll be gorgeous in winter." '

Marian looked away. She could hardly bear to hear what she knew was coming.

' "I've met this girl," he said.'

Marian sat down at Sally's feet, feeling dizzy.

'Was it a complete surprise?' she asked gently, but knowing the answer. Women like Sally never questioned their power. Why should they? She was shocked when Sally started to cry. She'd never heard her cry before in all the years she'd known her, couldn't even imagine such a thing.

'Tell me about it,' she said, wishing she could skip the next bit as she would in a novel. 'It'll do you good to talk. Tell me all about it.'

She went on repeating meaningless words and phrases, hardly conscious of what she was saying, while Sally's sobbing gradually reached the peak of desperation and suddenly subsided, leaving her sniffing and gasping for breath.

'That's better,' Marian said. 'That's much better. Good girl. Good girl.'

'But what a mess you've made of your face,' she added some time later, when she could bear to look at her. 'Come on. You must mop it up. Let me take you upstairs. I'll run a nice cool bath for you. My next door neighbour is coming in after supper. He saw that photograph of you and Virginia and he's dying to meet you. And you'll feel better for a bit of company. Come along.'

'I think I'd like to lie down for five minutes,' Sally said as she was shown into her room. 'I've been having pains in my back. My spine feels raw, a mass of raw nerves. I must lie down.'

'As long as you don't start to cry again,' Marian said, helping her into bed.

'I won't. I don't think so. I feel too exhausted.'

She gave Marian a little half-smile and touched her hand.

Marian went downstairs, feeling a great need to comfort and protect. Yes, Sally could be selfish and over-bearing and childish, goodness knows, but underneath she was warm-hearted and guileless and such an old friend. The sight of her eyes swamped with tears had moved her unbearably. She went to her desk and found the letter she'd recently had from her. "I'd like to come and stay for a while if you could have me. Virginia is spending the summer in Edinburgh so there's nothing to keep me here. Did I tell you that Alan has set up house with some young girl he met at his ciné club. C'est la vie." Etc.

No hint of the anguish.

Marian felt a spasm of anger towards Alan. How dared he? Everyone had been surprised that Sally had married him, thrown herself away on such a mild, insignificant little man, nothing but a background figure. Quite kind and dependable, she supposed, ready to do his share — and probably more than his share — in looking after Virginia when she was small, and decent, no doubt, in every other way. All the same, a nonentity. Earned a fair bit of money at some boring job in the city during the week, she wasn't even sure what he did, and gardened at the week-end.

Had Sally taken advantage of his good nature? Very probably. But he'd certainly seemed to thrive on it. The last time Marian had visited them in Highgate he'd seemed as devoted as ever. Quiet and shy and kind and devoted he'd seemed, picking things up at the delicatessen on his way home and insisting on doing most of the cooking. A small dark man, not unattractive, but a nobody. Men like Alan didn't suddenly leave women like Sally.

How I wish I'd bought some fresh salmon and some really good Chablis, she thought, as she sliced the stingy little pineapple and grilled the gammon. Gammon and mushrooms and supermarket wine seems so insensitive for a person with a broken heart.

In twenty minutes, supper ready, she went up to call Sally and found her lying on her back, mouth slightly opened, fast asleep. She shook her arm — surely Sally wouldn't want to sleep long, not on her first evening when there was so much to talk about — but could hardly rouse her. At last her eyes opened for a few seconds, 'Oh it's you, Marian,' she said, as she turned on her side, burrowing into the pillow in an even deeper sleep. Marian pulled the cotton bedspread over her, reluctantly deciding to leave her again.

As she went down the steep cottage stairs wondering how the meal could be re-heated later, she recognised the familiarity of the situation: she revising, postponing, scrapping plans to suit Sally. It had always been the same. She'd even changed the day originally fixed for her wedding because Sally had written to say she wouldn't be back from France till the following month. Dickie had been a little surprised, she remembered.

With a little shiver, she recalled the moment she'd first introduced Dickie to Sally. Her heart had been thumping. It was so important that they should like each other. Dickie, large and blonde and handsome — later he became a little too heavy — was presentable in every way, but what if Sally had thought him dull, trivial, or, even worse, a show-off. (He was six years older than she was, and at that time a fraction, perhaps, too sure of himself.) But no, it had been all right. She'd clowned about with him, which she never did with anyone she disliked and afterwards had pronounced that she approved. He had the right outlook on life, she'd said, a mature outlook, which was quite surprising in a medical student.

And when Marian had told her, a month or two later, that they were getting engaged, she'd hugged her and said she was a lucky old thing. Marian still remembered how the words had curled round her heart. She'd have married Dickie — surely she would — whatever Sally had thought of him, but there'd certainly have been a sizeable cloud in her mind.

'You're a lucky old thing.' Didn't she know it! She could hardly credit her good fortune. Not only was he tall and handsome with a square, strong face and lovely hands, but he was also very nearly a doctor. He and she had had bed-sitters in the same house in Chalk Farm for a while, and they'd met once or twice on the stairs and in the basement where the washing machine was, but she'd never expected him to notice her, let alone ask her out, let alone propose to her.

'Marian,' he'd said, and after such a short courtship, (people still had courtships in those days, how quaint it seemed now) 'Marian, would you consider marrying me?'

If she'd hesitated it was only to make sure that she'd heard properly. How could she have refused him? It was the perfect solution. She'd loved him, she assured herself, at least in a youthful, beribboned, bemused sort of way, but the over-riding beat in her heart was that it was a way out, a solution, that she could give up teaching: she'd never again have to face another class like 4F, another adversary like Kevin Pratt.

Teachers' training. It was a nightmare. Nothing in her placid, uneventful life had prepared her for that moment when she'd had to stand in front of those thirty-five hostile children all ready to pounce.

Oh, she knew the theories. You kept a class interested, fully occupied and motivated. You had all the facts at your finger-tips. Above all, you got into your stride as soon as you were inside the classroom door, before any pupil had had time to think of being unco-operative.

It didn't work. However quick you were, they were quicker. They'd had years and years of practice, your inexperience glowed like a halo round your unsuspecting head.

'Oh no, it's not *Language* today, Miss. You've got it wrong. It's *Drama* today. Mr Wilkinson promised us drama today.' 'We've got our pieces, Miss. We're supposed to be in the Hall today.' 'Oh Miss, Mr Wilkinson will be ever so annoyed. It's for the competition. We'll be letting him down. Well, don't say we didn't tell you.' 'What's your first name, Miss? Our last student said we could call her Carol, didn't she, Deb? Oh, all right, *be* like that.' 'My mother's got to go to hospital tomorrow, Miss. She's having an abortion. Do you believe in abortions, Miss?' 'Mrs Saunders doesn't, but it's OK for her, she doesn't have five kids, does she Miss?' 'She doesn't even have one.' 'She doesn't even have a husband anymore. He walked out on her.' 'Well if she shouted at him like she shouts at us, no wonder. Mean old cow.' 'Melanie Kirby had an abortion last year. Cross my heart and wish to die. A week before her fourteenth birthday. She said it was nothing, easier than having a tooth out, easier than a filling. Oh, Mandy Smith, you've got a dirty mind,you have.' 'My mother's got a prolapse.' 'My mother's got veins like great bunches of grapes. All down her thighs. I'm not having any bleedin' kids.' 'My auntie's been sterilised. They tie up your tubes.'

The girls chattered like gutter-sparrows.

The boys were not so talkative. But they were bigger.

He was a very big boy, Kevin Pratt; in size somewhere between a large man and a small gorilla. He had a low, rumbling voice and when bored had a tendency to pick up a chair and swing it round his head. He was always wanting metalwork.

He didn't take kindly to correction. 'It ain't fuckin' wrong,' he'd roar, 'I copied it from the bleedin' book.' (And the humiliation of a small girl in the front putting up her hand and offering to get a teacher.) 'It's bloody right, I tell you.' She got so that she was too nervous to cross out anything in his greasy rolled-up exercise book.

Dickie had saved her from 4F. Twenty years ago, she told herself, we might have been ashamed of marrying for money, but marrying to escape from the rigours of a career in teaching or nursing seemed perfectly permissible — and sensible. At least it meant we never felt trapped by marriage and babies like they do today. If I'd ever felt trapped, I'd only have to remember Kevin Pratt.

She was getting hungry. Emotion always made her hungry. Also she'd had very little time for lunch. Paul Dainton, who owned the antique shop she worked in, had been out at a sale that day, so she'd had a sandwich and a cup of tea without closing the shop. (Which was just as well because the couple who'd said they'd be back to look at a Persian rug had chosen that time to call and she'd managed to make a sale.)

What would Dickie think of her working at the antique shop, she wondered, as she often did. He used to dislike the shop saying everything in it was over-priced and poufy. He'd disliked Paul too, but she'd always had a soft spot for him and by this time had grown very fond of him. She liked the way he was so off-hand to his customers, especially the very rich ones who were used to having V.I.P. treatment. 'Yes, leave it. I should. I expect you've got several much better ones at home.'

She made herself a pot of tea and, feeling pleasantly virtuous, sipped two cups with no sugar and hardly any milk.

Then she found her will-power snapping like taut elastic and she cut herself a thick, spongy slice of fresh white bread. She didn't usually buy white bread because she couldn't leave it alone. Chocolate and cake she could resist, but not fresh white bread. She was almost a stone over-weight.

'I'm almost a stone over-weight,' she complained to her next-door neighbour when he called at exactly eight-thirty.

'Nonsense,' he said, as she knew he would. 'You're a perfect size. Just right. A womanly woman.'

Gerald Maitland was seventy years old and perhaps a bit of a bore. She'd asked him in because he loved meeting new people, especially women. There was no harm in him. She and Dickie had known him for years. He'd always looked after the cottage for them; opened windows, re-addressed letters, seen to burst pipes and falling tiles and once a six-foot burglar.

'I don't know whether to wake her or not,' she'd confided in him. 'She's unhappy and not very well. Perhaps it would be kinder to let her sleep.'

'Wake her. If she sleeps all evening she'll be awake at three and the small hours make everything worse. One's body is at its lowest ebb.'

'I'll give her another half-hour,' she said nervously.

'I saw you both walking up the hill, earlier.'

'I saw you watching us. Did you think her attractive?'

'Very. Good colouring. Good bones. I've got a feeling she'll settle here with you. I saw her looking around her several times as she walked up. Like a cat outside a new home.'

'Good Lord, I don't want her to settle here with me. It's never been considered. I've got no room for her. I've got to keep the spare room for the boys.'

'Put them in the attic. They're not often home.'

'Anyway, she wouldn't leave London. She leads a very full life.'

'It would be nice for you if she came. Now that you're both on your own. You could buy Paul's shop and manage it between you. Properly handled it could be a little gold-mine.'

'He's not selling the shop.'

'He would though, given half a decent offer. His heart's not in it these days. His boy-friend's got a nice little restaurant on the coast they tell me, quite a high-class place. Apparently Paul's dying to join him.'

'How do you know?'

'I put two and two together. You should come to the Farmers' Arms with me sometimes. I often see them there.'

To close the subject, about which his knowledge was entirely a matter of rumour and gossip, he pulled his gold half-hunter out of his waistcoat pocket and looked at it gravely.

He'd got his best suit on, Marian noticed with some amusement, and a tie she hadn't seen before; blue like his eyes. He was tall and elegant, but too thin now, his legs bony, his hands long and slender. An attractive man, his face brown, his hair silver-grey and thick, but twenty years too old for Sally.

All the same, Marian felt pleased with him. He looked a distinguished neighbour. And indeed he was distinguished; a retired University lecturer who'd written Sixth Form text books on Pre-History which were still in use and who from time to time gave lectures to some Royal Society in London. And as though that weren't enough, nowadays often appeared on television in connection with his recent researches into the siting of Celtic barrows and standing stones. Sally, always more intellectual than she was, would be impressed by him.

'She looks a strong personality,' he said, turning his eyes to the ceiling. 'Forceful. Dynamic.'

'Dickie used to say she bullied me,' Marian said. 'And I suppose she does.'

'That's neither here nor there if you really like her.'

'Oh I do.'

She thought of a night just before Johnny's birth, over twenty years ago. (Sally herself was about three months pregnant and still at the sick stage.) Dickie was on night duty at Casualty. 'You know exactly what to do if anything starts,' he'd said, kissing the top of her head as he'd left. 'I know you won't panic. After all, you're a doctor's wife.' She could remember the complacent note in his voice, and later the sound of his car driving away.

She'd immediately had a stomach ache, convinced herself that it was the beginning of labour...and panicked.

She'd phoned Sally who lived about eight miles away in North London and she'd left everything and come over in a terrible old car she could hardly drive, willing and ready to sympathise, time contractions and help her relax. The stomach ache had turned out to be wind and they'd spent a lovely evening making pancakes which was one of the things Sally had to eat to keep the sickness at bay. (The buttery smell of pancakes and the tang of lemon still reminded her of that evening.) Sally had phoned Alan to say she'd be staying over-night and they'd played old records and danced and laughed till long past midnight. And it wasn't until six o'clock the next morning, when Dickie had arrived home, that her labour pains had really started. He'd had very little sleep, she remembered, with some satisfaction.

'It's nine o'clock,' Gerald said, glancing at his watch again, 'And I think you should call her. What's the matter with her anyway? What's a divorce nowadays?'

'She can't seem to accept it.'

'She can't be short of friends. Doesn't she have a job? A career?'

Marian, nervous of all the disloyalties she might be guilty of, wished he'd go home, or at least stop questioning her.

'She has a job,' she said. 'Of course she has. She went back to work when Virginia was about six months old.'

'You didn't approve of that. I can tell by the little sniff in your voice.'

'It was nothing to do with me. She had quite an adequate nanny for the first few years and then a succession of au-pairs.'

'Poor Virginia.'

'Why poor Virginia?'

'That's what you were implying, surely.'

'Not at all...Well, not exactly. Alan's mother lived quite near them. She helped a lot.'

'What does she do now?'

'She's dead. She died about ten years ago.'

'Marian, what does *Sally* do now?'

'She teaches drama in a Polytechnic. Not that it's ever meant all that much to her; teaching. At least she never talks about it. She's involved with quite an ambitious amateur dramatic company, though. She's probably more interested in that. I used to go and see her when she had a leading part.'

'Was she good?'

Marian sighed. 'I could never be sure. You know how I am, I'm never sure about anything.'

Gerald looked hard at her until she continued. 'Well, she was very spirited, but just a bit embarrassing somehow.'

'What a pity she never did it professionally. If she could put heart and soul into her work she wouldn't have the energy to worry about anything else.'

'Oh, don't be silly Gerald,' Marian said. She was suddenly fed up with his easy solutions to every problem. (When Dickie died, he'd tried to persuade her to do another degree.) She was fed up with him for being a man and having no problems.

'I'm not being silly. Do you honestly think a surgeon, for instance, about to start on a critical operation, has time to worry about any personal problems he may have?'

16

'No, but by the time he's finished and washing his hands they probably come flooding back to him again. No-one keeps their full attention on their work for very long. About five minutes an hour is the average, I should think.'

'Nonsense. My work absorbed me. It still does.'

'You were very lucky.'

'Indeed I was.'

Everything about him angered her. His complacency was sickening, and his extreme curiosity about Sally, simply because she was sexually attractive, seemed quite indecent.

'So was your wife,' she said. 'She could be unfaithful to you, knowing that you were so absorbed in your work that you wouldn't turn a hair.'

'She was never unfaithful to me.'

'How can you possibly know? You were always absorbed in your work.'

'Some women you can trust implicitly. My wife was one. You're another. I'm quite certain that Dickie always had absolute trust in you.'

Marian, while acknowledging the truth of this, wished it wasn't so obvious. It wasn't as though she wore vests or ankle socks. (But even quite frivolous clothes looked sensible on her.)

'Did you have a mistress?' she asked him.

'A mistress? Certainly not.'

'You were never unfaithful to your wife?' (It was Alan she wished to punish.)

'That's an entirely different matter.'

'So you were! Well, I knew you were. She told me so.'

Gerald sat up straighter in his chair. 'You're teasing me,' he said.

To Marian's dismay, his eyes were half-closed as though to stave off a blow.

'Of course I am,' she said hurriedly.

She was. Gerald's wife had died before Marian had had a chance of getting to know her at all well — though several other women had been only too eager to speak on her behalf. A secretary at the British Museum, the wife of an Oxford don, a woman M.P., all had been reported to Marian as being closer to Gerald than his married state warranted.

'I think I can hear Sally getting up,' she said.

Gerald Maitland pressed back his hair and straightened his tie.

TWO

A snatch of sleep had done wonders for Sally. When she came downstairs her eyes looked rested and her skin was glowing. She had changed into a grey silk dress and her chestnut brown hair had been brushed back and lay docile on the nape of her neck.

Gerald became another man with another voice. He's puffing out his chest feathers, Marian thought, as she introduced him to Sally. And well he might. She's still a stunner in spite of that rather long nose that used to worry her so much.

Sally sat with her hands in her lap looking demure, letting Marian and Gerald do the talking. It was not ever thus, thought Marian, remembering how Sally's volatile personality used to dominate every gathering. Tonight, she seemed only half awake.

It was when Gerald was telling her about the formation of the Preseli mountain range which they could see in the distance; how they were igneous masses isolated by the excoriation of the Great Ice Age that Sally's smile started to slip and Marian rushed five hundred million years to her aid.

'Oh Heavens,' she said, 'I haven't given her anything to eat. Gerald, you must excuse us. She'll be starving.'

'I'm all right,' Sally said.

'I've got some gammon steaks and pineapple. I'll have to wrap them in foil and re-heat them.'

'They'll be ruined,' Gerald said firmly. 'Dry and salty. I'll take you out to the Castle for some sea-food. Come along.' He stood up, young and determined.

'Oh no,' Marian said, 'Honestly Gerald, I'm too tired. I'm not dressed.'

Sally said nothing.

'Nonsense. Just put your white coat over the top and come along. It'll do you both good.'

Being Tuesday, the lounge bar of the hotel was half empty. Gerald ushered them to the window-table as though over a red carpet at the

Ritz.

'And what has the chef got for us tonight?' he asked the little ginger-haired barmaid who came for their order. 'Lobster thermidor? Sole en Goujons? Crab mousse?'

'Now Mr Maitland, you know as well as I do, it's only Mrs Lloyd and it's scampi and chips or sea-food platter.'

'Scampi and chips will do excellently. With green salad perhaps?'

'Perhaps,' the little barmaid said, writing their order on the back of a beer mat. 'Unless Ivor's had all the lettuce again. He got upstairs this morning. Quite upset the lady in Number Five. Carafe of white, is it?'

'No, not the house wine, not tonight. We'll have some of your Muscadet '86. Mr Lloyd knows which one.'

'Muscadet '86' she repeated, appraising Sally as she wrote. 'Right you are then.'

The locals liked Gerald well enough. He was always ready to stand them a round, and, though scorning his romantic notions about the standing stones and tombs and other features of the landscape they'd taken for granted since childhood, they enjoyed seeing him on the telly. Anecdotes about him, most of them apocryphal, abounded. Many were about his clothes, how he got his shirts from Jermyn Street and, according to some, his panama hats from Panama, others about his cars; for all his degrees he knew less than a woman about an engine. 'Aye, he got Bert out one morning because the Merc. wouldn't start and you know what the trouble was, don' you?' Their laughter was kindly; oiled by the money they made out of him.

Her earlier anger forgotten, Marian now felt very sorry for Gerald. He was arranging things so nicely and Sally was behaving like someone in a trance, smiling like the Mona Lisa, and saying little more, so that she was having to be warmer and more enthusiastic than she wanted to be, which meant that he'd probably get the wrong idea once again.

Not that Gerald seemed aware of Sally's vacant expression. He went on talking like the narrator of a travelogue about the mountains of the area, the rivers, cliffs and coastline, seeming not to need more than the occasional, 'Is that so?' from Marian who had heard it all before, many times.

As for Gerald, he was wishing that his friend Councillor Reg Ward would come in and catch sight of him from the bar. Not that he'd introduce them, Reg being a rough sort of fellow, but he'd like, all the same, to meet his eye. He'd always enjoyed the company of pretty women and these two were more than pretty — both of them. Marian was plump and glossy and had the kind of looks he liked best. He liked an olive skin, rather moist, and warm brown eyes. He liked the way her dark hair was pulled back from her face — you needed good bones for that style. He liked the untouched streaks of grey in her hair. Most of all he liked the way she pretended interest in his lengthy dissertation, when he knew she was bored out of her mind. If he were only twenty years, ten years younger, he told himself, he'd insist on taking her on, in spite of those near-delinquent sons of hers. Or was he fooling himself as usual? Wasn't it Mrs Rushton — Sally — that he'd really go for? When had he ever been able to resist the challenge of the Beauty, however cold or vain she might be. Just occasionally he was glad to be seventy and out of it. Or was he fooling himself again?

He signalled to the little barmaid. 'Coffee, please,' he said. 'A pot of coffee and three brandies.'

'Brandies, is it,' she said, her pale eyebrows shooting up.

'Well, this has been a pleasant evening. Such a treat for me. Marian takes pleasure in friendship. You'd be surprised, Mrs Rushton, how much she's appreciated in this little town.'

Sally raised her eyes and looked at Marian. 'I'm sure she is,' she murmured, looking surprised.

'Really, Gerald, what nonsense,' Marian said with a little giggle. 'I don't know anyone, I don't go anywhere. What's all this about? Who, apart from you, and possibly the Daintons, would care if I packed up and left this little town tomorrow?'

'She's kind and good and understanding, Mrs Rushton. Good and kind. "A lady sweet and kind." How does the song go?'

'"I did but see her passing by. And yet I love her till I die,"' Sally said obligingly.

'That's right, that's right. "And yet I love her till I die." Absolutely right. Spot on, as they say these days. And now I ought to take you home, my dears, because I know Marian likes to get to bed by eleven. And perhaps, Mrs Rushton, Sally I mean, you'll allow me to take you round the town tomorrow when Marian's at the shop. Shall I call for you at half past ten? An early start? Excellent, excellent, I'll look forward to that.'

'He's rather pompous,' Marian said apologetically when she and Sally were back in the house. 'Harmless, though, and very lonely. All the same, I know I shouldn't have inflicted him on you on your first evening.'

It was cool at last. A tiny breeze ruffled the curtains as she drew them. She hoped the weather would break.

'I don't think I can bear it,' Sally said, coming to stand in front of her and clutching her tightly round the arms. 'You must help me. I'm going out of my mind.'

Her voice broke. The tears ran down her face in a steady stream.

'I *will* help you,' Marian said, leading her to a chair and getting her to sit. 'I *will*. Let's thrash this out. I want to help you. I *will*.'

She thought of Sally visiting her in the hospital a few hours after Johnny was born — white wine thoughtfully decanted into a Luco-zade bottle — the way she'd bounced on the bed and been as excited as she was. No-one forgot the birth of their first baby. Sally was a part of that best time of her life.

'Darling,' she said gently, 'you must come to terms with what's happened. After all, it's a such common occurrence. Men are forever falling in love with younger women and leaving their wives. It's not fair, no. But life isn't fair is it? It wasn't fair that you were so beautiful and Emma Marie Coates so plain. She couldn't help her looks, could she? She was much more in love with Alan than you ever were and he never as much as noticed her. That wasn't fair either.'

'I'd forgotten Emma Marie Coates,' Sally said.

'So has everyone. She was good-natured and intelligent, but she hadn't a chance, poor creature, not a breath of a chance; terrible skin, small breasts, bumpy nose, thin legs. I remember her being so brave about it too. "There are thousands of people worse off than me," she used to say. To my shame, I could hardly think of one. She teaches at a girls' boarding school in Malvern or somewhere. She'll go on until she retires, getting a bit stricter and a bit more spiteful every year. She's had nothing, not even memories.'

'She's probably a dedicated careerist,' Sally said. 'That's what every woman wants to be these days.'

'But only when they've sampled everything else, having men and babies and so on. It's OK afterwards but not before.'

A grey suede moth fluttered into the room, bumping into the table lamp.

'Anyway,' Marian continued, (she'd prepared her line of argument in the pub whilst hanging on to Gerald's every word) 'it wasn't as though you stayed at home behaving yourself and being a good little wife. That would have made things much more unfair. If you're honest with yourself, you'll admit that you led Alan a hell of a dance.'

'I know I did,' Sally said in a small voice. 'I'm not proud of it.'

'But it evens things up, doesn't it? I mean, you spoke of being humiliated. I don't see how you can.'

'He understood that I needed to break out sometimes.'

'All the same, he must have minded. He probably suffered deeply.'

'He didn't seem to. Did he ever say anything to you?'

'No. But he wouldn't have said anything to me. We were never close, I was *your* friend.'

'He didn't seem to mind. He used to tease me about it. "That poor devil's hooked," he used to say. "What's the score now?" It all meant nothing. It was a game. I didn't realise how useless and silly it was. It's taken me twenty years to understand myself and the sad thing is, it's too late. We go through life gaining experience — and a certain amount of wisdom, I suppose — and what's it all for? We could live so sanely and decently if we could have a second go at it.'

Marian rescued the moth and put it out.

'I begged him not to leave me,' Sally said. 'I told him he could have as many affairs as he wanted.'

She started to tremble so violently that it was some time before she could go on speaking. 'He just looked through me,' she said. 'Just looked through me and started packing his clothes.'

'You've had a terrible shock,' Marian said, moved by Sally's words, but trying to speak softly and calmly. 'You depended on him. You didn't dream he could let you down, and he did.'

'I thought he'd always be there when I needed him. I put my trust in him.'

'It will take you a long time to get over it. But you will.'

'I try, but I can't.'

'You will. I thought I'd never be able to accept Dicky's death. For months I couldn't believe it. He hadn't been ill in his life. Why should a man of forty-five suddenly have a colossal heart-attack? I couldn't take it in.'

Sally had stopped listening to her. 'At least, I've been able to talk to someone at last,' she said. 'Up to now, I've tried to make light of it, telling people we'd decided to split up. I've never been able to face the truth.'

22

'It's the first part of acceptance,' Marian said.

They sat in silence for a few minutes.

It was past midnight when Marian took Sally up the narrow staircase to her room.

The low cottage bedroom suddenly seemed bare and ugly. She'd taken down the various posters of unprepossessing young men with guitars and drums, pinned up by the boys over the years, but had put nothing on the dirty, yellowing walls in their place. How she wished she'd had the room re-decorated for Sally. Why hadn't she at least picked some roses? It struck her that the plant she'd carried up from the front porch where it was getting too much sun, was exactly the same nasty colours as the Indian bedcover; squashed plum and mud-green.

'It's a lovely room,' Sally said, 'So masculine. I haven't slept in a room like this for years.'

'The boys used to share it,' Marian said, her spirits immediately reviving, 'But now Tim has the attic. Not that either of them is home for very long; just enough time to dump their dirty washing in the Keymatic, then they're off again. They're at some rock festival at the moment.'

'Have you got a photograph of them? It's years since I saw them.'

Her tiredness forgotten, Marian went to her room, bringing back a large framed photograph.

'They *are* handsome,' Sally said looking at them closely. 'John looks more like Dicky than ever. And Tim, who ever does he look like? Not a bit like either of you.'

Marian took the photograph from Sally and sighed over Tim.

'Tim' she said. 'Oh, he's very lazy and good-for nothing. He went to Manchester Poly because he wanted to be near John, but he failed all his first year exams and was kicked out. He says he's going to go on Social Security in September. "You can surely get some sort of job," I said. But he didn't think he should compete for the one or two vacancies that come up in the Highways Department — I think that means road sweeping — it didn't seem fair, he said. I think he's just perfectly happy doing nothing. I keep trying to tell myself that it's a phase, but honestly, he's always been the same. He's never wanted to do anything. What will happen when he wants to get married and have a family?'

'But Marian, he's only nineteen. He's got plenty of time. If he's not academic, perhaps he's the artistic type.'

Marian sighed again. 'No. He was keen on photography for about a week last summer. So I bought him a really expensive camera for his birthday. But he's probably sold it by this time. Or given it away. He's very good-natured.'

'He always was. I adored Tim. So did Virginia.'

'Yes, she did. She was nearer John in age, but it was Tim she always wanted to play with.'

'They were going to get married. Do you remember?'

Marian sighed even more deeply. 'I remember the day Virginia told him it was all off,' she said. 'She was staying with us — you and Alan had gone to Crete I think — they were talking in the kitchen and I was ironing and pretending not to listen, "You know we've always said we'd get married," she said in a very brisk voice, "Well, children always say things like that. What will really happen is that we'll meet someone else and marry them instead." "Will we?" Tim said. "Oh, I see." That's all he said. "Oh, I see." But he was really heart-broken. I can see his little face now. A dead look in his eyes. It was probably the turning-point in his life. The time he gave up.'

'Oh, don't be silly, Marian. How old was he?'

'About eight. It was terrible. I could have killed Virginia.'

'She was only being honest.'

'Oh, she was honest, all right. But I've never really cherished that sort of honesty, have you?'

'No,' Sally said. 'I've met this girl.'

'And I bet he's regretted it already,' Marian said crossly, realising that they were back where they'd started. 'And serve him right, too. Try to feel angry with him, Sally. He's a stupid idiot, that's what he is. Say that twenty-five times before you go to sleep.'

THREE

The sun was already hot when Marian woke the next morning, the sky already a vivid mid-day blue. She had her breakfast — black coffee and Ryvita that day to atone for the chips of the previous evening — on the patio behind the house.

Patio, she said to herself derisively, some patio. Eleven or twelve flag-stones set between the back door and the coalhouse. This is a backyard this is, in spite of my efforts — the black and white barrels of hydrangea petiolaris (blue) and the scarlet geraniums and the small headless statue reputed to have come from a manor house near Milford Haven — a small backyard and beyond it a crumbling white-washed wall.

Oh, but it wasn't too bad. She took a deep breath. The honey-smell of the alyssum which grew everywhere, even on the wall, mingled with the musky smell of geranium and catmint. The hot bees bumbled about heavy as little buses. A peacock butterfly sunned itself on the slightly concave back step.

She looked up at the house. Not even an estate agent could have made it sound impressive. It wasn't highly desirable, deceptively spacious or abounding in olde worlde charm, and the garden was neither well laid out nor labour-saving.

What it was was a small plain grey cottage, originally a two up, two down; four windows and a door in the front, built almost three hundred years ago to keep out the weather. Two additional rooms had been added in the Thirties; a sizeable kitchen downstairs and a bathroom above, some years ago they themselves had made a third bedroom out of the loft space. The sloping garden to the side of the house was laid out like a tea plantation; four pocket-handkerchief sized lawns on different levels and a straggling orchard — with washing line — at the top.

Why had she decided to settle here rather than in the large Victorian house in Ealing which had been her home for twenty years? Dickie's partner had offered to buy the Ealing house, complete with furniture and fixtures, that was why; she usually did what seemed easiest. Also, Dickie had loved the cottage and she'd somehow felt closer to him there, felt it was where she was meant to be. She still felt that. Perhaps that was the real reason.

At first, the boys had been annoyed with her decision to leave London, but she'd pointed out that it wouldn't affect them for long; John was already seventeen and Tim fifteen when their father died, and they'd soon accepted it and settled down.

She was reasonably happy, she supposed, with reasonably interesting neighbours and a reasonably interesting job. What more could she expect? What more did she want, come to that? It was only Sally's arrival, Sally's discontent that had made her restless.

If she married Gerald, would she be happier? He was sure she would. And intelligent companionship, she told herself, wasn't to be sneezed at. Would the boys mind? Of course they wouldn't mind. They wouldn't turn a hair if she told them she was going to emigrate to Australia. John would pat her back encouragingly as though she were the child and he the parent. Perhaps Tim's eyes would darken for a moment or two.

Oh God, when he was two and prone to nightmares and Dickie wouldn't have him in their bed, she used to sit up half the night by his cot holding his hand. Once, she'd fallen asleep when he had, and all the next morning she'd had the deep marks of the cot rail on her cheeks. Why had she suddenly thought of that?

You'd think they'd give you something back for all that love. No, it was one-way traffic, you had to face it. Oh God, but it could make you cry if you let it. The memories. Little sticky hands that wanted nothing but to hold yours. The hot breath, kisses, tears on your cheeks.

Heavens above, she'd gone through all this when they'd left home, surely she wasn't going to suffer it all again. Post-natal depression. Only it hit her twenty years late. They're strong and healthy and moderately law-abiding, she told herself, and once in a while they remember to ring me. It's just as it should be.

One day she'd have grandchildren perhaps. She suddenly had a vision of Tim and Virginia together as they used to be. Wishful thinking, she told herself. Only because she and Sally had talked about them last night. All the same, if they met again after — how many years was it — mightn't they fall in love? Far stranger things happened.

Virginia would be so right for Tim. She was so strong and clever, a little like Sally but far more serious and purposeful. True, she was living with someone at the moment, but he sounded such a boor and Tim was gentle and sensitive.

She'd try to get Virginia down when he was next home. John could manage for himself, he was like Dickie so sensible and practical. At fourteen, left a hundred pounds in his grandmother's will, he'd started researching banks and building societies, making graphs about different charges and interest rates and guaranteed returns. Then it was press-ups and jogging and calorie-contolled diet; raw vegetables, roughage and no white sugar. No wonder he was so thin. Though Tim, it must be said, was as wondrously thin on sweet tea, chips and baked beans and lying down flat on his back watching television.

The church clock striking the half hour brought her back to the present. She dried her eyes, threw away her cold coffee and went back to the house.

Sally kept her eyes closed as Marian tip-toed to her bedroom door to see if she was awake and breathed a sigh of relief as she turned to go downstairs.

There was something about Marian that brought out the worst in her, making her feel guilty and inadequate. She'd got quite huffy about this being her first visit to the cottage, but there'd never been room in it for two families, and she could never tolerate the idea of roughing it. And how could she have come to comfort her over Dickie's death when she was suffering far more herself? Marian had never really loved him. Oh yes, she'd married him happily enough, triumphantly even, but all she'd ever wanted was a husband, a father for her children. Not Dickie.

She wouldn't let herself think about Dickie. It was foolish to plague herself over something that was past. It wasn't as if their affair had ever impinged on Marian's life. Marian was oblivious to the fact that they were anything but friends, was completely taken in by the teasing, bantering relationship which was all they could permit themselves in front of her.

How was it that Marian had never suspected anything? She knew they met in town from time to time. Was it her innate goodness? Was she simply unable to comrehend that either her husband or her friend was capable of the least disloyalty? Let alone the ultimate betrayal?

No, Sally preferred to think that she was simply too engrossed in her children and her cosy domesticity, that she was not in love with Dickie, at least not so bound to him that she was aware of his every thought and mood, even those, particularly those, he tried to hide from her.

Love was a terrible thing. Marian had been lucky to escape it. She, Sally, had loved Dickie to madness, had suffered fire every time he looked at another woman in that certain way he had; the swift, half-smiling glance, head to one side. Torment.

Of course there'd been the pleasure as well. She felt her nipples grow hard, her thighs relax as she thought of it. There was no limit to the attention he'd been prepared to pay to her body, as a lover he was thorough, decisive, intense. She moaned as she remembered. All the passion of ten years.

They'd been very careful to keep it secret, but hadn't been altogether succesful. She suddenly remembered one of Virginia's birthday parties, probably her sixteenth. Marian had come over bringing John and Timothy and for some reason Dickie had come too. Alan was home and the four of them had escaped the noise and gone to the pub for a couple of hours and then had sat in the kitchen eating crisps and cheese straws and drinking vodka. And somehow it had all seemed friendly and innocent that night, Alan and Dickie surprisingly comfortable together.

But at about two in the morning after everybody had been persuaded to go home and she was getting ready for bed, Virginia had looked in on her. 'You and Dickie are having an affair aren't you,' she'd said; less a question than a statement, neither surprise nor anger in her voice.

'Whatever makes you think that?' Sally had asked, stalling for time.

'I've known for ages. I suppose everybody knows but Marian.'

It had seemed almost friendly, not at all an accusation. All the same, she'd had tears in her eyes. She idolized Marian. Most people were quite fond of her, but Virginia idolized her.

But she hadn't broken up the marriage, Sally told herself, hadn't taken him away from Marian. Though there were days, nights, when she'd come within a breath of it.

She mustn't think of him. He was dead. And three years and five months later she still couldn't stop her heart pounding, her stomach churning at the shock of it.

She had been numb and tearless for weeks and weeks. And Alan had stood by her and comforted her. He had accepted that Dickie was the love of her life and had been a staunch friend. He had become important to her. Yes, she might have had one or two affairs since Dickie's death, but they hadn't counted. Nothing had counted but Dickie...She mustn't think of Dickie.

If Alan had left her while she was still with Dickie, she could have understood it, could have accepted it. At that time he used to say he was staying because of Virginia, but that cut no ice with her. She knew that men weren't ruled by their duty but by their pricks. He used to say often enough that life with her was hell, but it was the sort of hell men put up with if there was a bit of the other with it. No, he'd stayed with her because he desired her and he'd left her because he'd stopped desiring her. It was as simple as that.

She was too angry to cry. It wasn't as if she'd let herself go, as women did in magazine stories. She hadn't put on weight, not an ounce, since she was in her twenties. Her doctor prescibed hormones, she spent a fortune on aromatherapy and vitamin tablets and royal-jelly capsules and ginseng and hours on bloody boring aerobics. She didn't touch alcohol except when there seemed no alternative but suicide.

And yet some vital ingredient in her make-up was drying up.

Virginia said it was a sense of proportion. But it was all right for her. She was just twenty and living with some sort of pop artist who was handsome and arrogant and a bit of a swine. And she had all her life in front of her.

Virginia was at university in Newcastle, chosen because it put four hours' journey between herself and her parents. She had had enough of them both, particularly her mother. She hardly ever phoned these days. Perhaps she still phoned Alan.

Sally couldn't phone Alan in case his girl-friend answered. Hannah. Who was an infants' teacher. Who studied astronomy and Gaelic in her spare time. Who was twenty-five.

Sally was too agitated to get back to sleep. She got up, had a bath, drank some lemon juice and got dressed. Gerald Maitland would be calling for her in just over an hour.

Gerald Maitland. Was Marian thinking of marrying him, she wondered. Perhaps they'd get on very well. He looked rich and rather distinguished and Marian had always been old before her time. He'd got a beautiful house apparently and Marian surely couldn't go on living in a two-bedroomed farm labourer's cottage indefinitely. Without a fitted kitchen or a cloakroom or a proper shower.

She wandered into Marian's bedroom — *Woman and Home* floral chintz — and came face to face with a large framed photograph of Dickie. He looked handsome, but smug and self-satisfied. She remembered the look so well. The smugness. She saw him standing in front of a mirror getting into his shirt, thick legs, strong knees still bare, then putting his tie on, his trousers, his jacket; getting ready to go again.

He'd never been prepared to leave Marian.

Bastard, she said, throwing the frame to the floor. She fell onto Marian's bed, pounding the pillows with her fists.

She was down, right down and she couldn't seem to pull herself up. Until the last few years she'd been a proud, assertive, independent woman, scornful of those who floundered. She'd found it almost impossible to turn to someone for comfort and help, but that is what she'd done. She'd turned to Alan, the husband who had once promised to love and cherish her. And he'd forsaken her. She hated him.

Or did she love him? She didn't know. She didn't know anything except that she wanted him back, needed him back, needed his support. She felt she'd go mad, raving mad, if he didn't come back to her.

Or was she already mad? She certainly couldn't seem to contol her thoughts these days, was aware only of a turbulence where she went pitching from darkness to darkness.

And her body was growing older, minute by desperate minute and she could do nothing to stop it happening. At last, oh, it would crumble to dust, but perhaps *this* was the most terrifying part; the loss of power, the loss of power.

For some minutes she lay on the bed, biting her knuckles.

Then she dried her eyes on the top sheet and looked out at the distant hills.

And gradually she grew calmer, picked up the photograph from the floor — it wasn't damaged — and put it to her cheek

Marian had tip-toed in to see Sally before she left for the shop, but finding her fast asleep, had decided not to wake her.

As she went past Gerald's gate she thought she'd better have a further word with him about the gravity of Sally's condition.

'Don't worry about her,' he said. 'What she needs is a lot of sympathy and a lot of re-assurance. I'll do what I can. You may count on me. You know that.'

She knew that.

'Come in for a minute,' he said, seeing that she was making no move to go. 'I'm having my breakfast. Join me for a cup of coffee.'

'Thank you,' she said, following him into the house. 'There's nothing much doing at the shop on a Wednesday. I might have stayed home if Sally was up.'

What a lovely house Gerald had. It was late Georgian or early Regency, she could never remember which, and so gracious, the rooms exactly the right size. And it was furnished so simply, so harmoniously that you never noticed any particular piece, or at least she didn't.

The breakfast-room at the back of the house overlooked the garden which had recently been landscaped by some London firm, but looked very pretty all the same. No rose bushes of course or anything as common as delphiniums or phlox (her favourites) but curving paths and low walls and clipped shrubs and a trickling stream called a water-course.

'I don't suppose I can tempt you to a piece of toast,' Gerald said as he passed her a cup of deliciously strong coffee.

'Perhaps one piece,' Marian said. 'If it won't be robbing you. Is it sliced white?'

'I'm afraid so.'

'It's my favourite. Silver-shred marmalade? Delicious. The Whole-Health stuff I get is really nasty. Not that I even had that this morning.'

'You should always allow yourself time for a good breakfast.'

'You're the only person I know who still uses these huge white napkins. Who cleans your silver?'

Gerald refused to hear her. 'I think there's some ulterior motive for this call,' he said.

Marian shot him a hurt glance, then chewing delicately, looked out again at the garden.

He changed his tactics. 'Won't you tell me what's on your mind, dear?'

'I only came about Sally — honestly — but seeing the garden looking so splendid...'

'Yes.'

'I wondered why you haven't had a party this year. You give such super parties. And the weather is so gorgeous at the moment. We could have a buffet supper laid out here, little tables outside, lights in the trees.'

'We?' Gerald said.

'I'd help. I'd be pleased to. You could ask some of those television people you had last Christmas. Justin Somebody. Sheila Ford-Smith. She was very nice I thought, seemed very fond of you. Do you still see her?'

'From time to time. You're not trying to marry me off, are you? I'm not being a particular nuisance, am I?'

'Of course not.'

'You're trying to fix Sally up with a presentable young chap, is that it? An up-and-coming television director? Marian, I'm not against the idea of a party, but I'd appreciate being in on whatever scheme you're hatching. I'd be able to be of much more use to you, for one thing.'

Marian finished her triangle of toast and took another.

'I'd like to get Virginia down,' she said, after she'd buttered it. 'She really should spend some time with Sally. And she'd come for a party. You know what youngsters are like, they simply don't see things until they're shoved right into the middle of them.'

'As long as she doesn't bring a van-load of North-country under-graduates with her,' Gerald said.

'That sounds a bit racist, Gerald. Look, what if I promise to sleep them all, however many she brings?'

'In your cottage?'

'They don't ask for much space, fair play to them. Just enough for their sleeping bags. I'll cope.'

Gerald shrugged his shoulders, accepting, with some reluctance, a student influx .

'Paul and his boy-friend?' he asked.

'Of course. The girls from the library. Miss Edwards and her cellist. Bob and Mary Vaughan. Hilda. The Tripps.'

'Will your boys be home?'

'Gerald, there's no need for that voice. I think the Festival is more or less over, but I don't know what their plans are after that. They may come home. I hope so. They seem able to behave fairly decently at parties, don't they?'

'Marian, I'll do anything for you except pretend that your sons seem able to behave fairly decently at parties. They do not. However, since they are your sons, I shall have to make the best of it and try to welcome them.'

'Thank you, Gerald. So when do you think would be the best day? Would Saturday suit you?'

'This Saturday? Good Lord, no. That's much too soon.'

'It would be a shame to miss the good weather.'

'But there's a great deal to be done, Marian. A party requires careful organisation.'

'I often think the best parties are the unorganised ones, though. The ones that just happen. No? What about Sunday, then? That gives us four whole days to phone people and order the drinks. Or even next Saturday?'

'I'll think about it and let you know this evening.'

'Thank you, Gerald. It'll cheer Sally up no end. Honestly. She'll probably get herself a new dress from Christine's.'

'You should get one, too. Poor Christine's doing very badly, she tells me.'

'Serves her right. She only stocks the tiniest sizes. I mean, size 14 isn't exactly gross, is it? Well, I'd better be off, I suppose. Thank you for my nice breakfast.'

When Marian pushed open the door of the shop shortly after ten o'clock, Paul Dainton got to his feet, mumbled something and hastily closed the top of his desk.

'Love letters?' she asked him, 'Or just another pornographic magazine?'

'I wasn't expecting you this morning. You startled me. Didn't your friend arrive?'

'Yes, she arrived all right.'

He smiled, waiting for her to continue.

'She's in a bit of a state, that's all. Gerald Maitland's volunteered to look after her this morning.'

'And that's all you're going to tell me? I'm not mature enough for women's matters, is that it? See if I care.'

He strutted over to the window pretending to be offended.

'You noticed that I sold the rug,' she said, ignoring, as always, his lapses into campery. 'That nice young couple came back. I gave them a receipt for nineteenth century Hamadan. I hope we won't be sued.'

Paul was handsome in profile. He had a long face, a long thin nose and close-cropped hair. In full face, his eyes were rather small and his mouth slack. On the whole, though, a good face; Roman rather than English.

'*Was* it a nineteenth century Hamadan?' she asked. 'Or even a Hamadan?'

He shrugged his shoulders a little more than was necessary. 'Search me,' he said. 'One book says one thing, one another. It looked pretty old — faded and worn — they may have got themselves a bargain. I couldn't care.'

'You ought to care,' Marian said. 'If you have ambitions to set up as an antique dealer rather than a purveyor of junk you jolly well ought to care. You have a reputation to build up.'

'I know, I know,' he said roughly, these being grounds they went over all too often. 'But building up a reputation could take more time than I can spare.'

'How's Gareth?' she asked after a moment or two and in a gentler voice. 'And how come everyone seems to have met him but me?'

'We're going through hell at the moment.'

'Oh dear,' Marian said. 'There seems so much of it about.'

Marian was about to pick up a duster to show that her working day had officially begun, when three elderly ladies — visitors to the town — trooped into the shop. They looked despondent, as though holidays weren't all they were cracked up to be, perhaps they'd had a quarrel about incidental expenses, perhaps their sensible low-heeled sandals were too new. Even inside the shop they went on fanning themselves with their tourists' brochures, as though the bright sunshine outside was the last straw.

Paul, who thought customers the really deadly thing about the antique business, retired to his desk.

Marian stepped towards them, smiling. 'Can I help you? Are you looking for anything in particular? Or do you just want to browse?'

'Tipstaves,' one of the women said in a breathy voice. 'Tipstaves. Are we going to be in luck?' She was very large, her white and gold dress, made of some material like furnishing brocade, under such strain that Marian was almost afraid to take her eyes off it.

'I'm afraid not,' she said. 'You see, we tend to specialise in oak furniture, Persian and Oriental rugs and antiquarian books. We haven't a single tiptrave at the moment.'

'What a dear little duck,' exclaimed the second woman, small and neat in mauve. 'I think perhaps my grand-daughter would like this for her birthday. Is it very expensive, dear?'

'We had several of these jelly moulds once,' the third lady, navy floral and pearls, said in a piercing whisper. 'I couldn't be doing with them. Threw the whole lot out.'

'Not for what it is,' Marian said. 'Two pounds seventy-five.'

'Think of the bacteria in that crazing. Germ jelly, that's what you'd be eating.'

The small woman was surveying the small duck from all angles. She turned it over as though to determine its sex. 'Does that include the VAT?' she asked.

'Yes, VAT is included on all items.'

'It's very pretty,' she said, turning it over once more, 'But no, I don't think I'll have it. You see, I thought it would be more expensive. I couldn't give my grand-daughter something costing two pounds seventy-five. She's a Queen's Guide.'

'What about this porcelain cherub?' Marian suggested. 'Mid-Victorian and in beautiful condition, not a chip or scratch. And as you can see, the gilding is perfect. Fifteen pounds fifty. Quite a bargain.'

'Are cherubs collectable?' the lady in navy threw at her, adding in another stage whisper, 'Hideous, if you want my opinion. Wouldn't give it house-room.'

'Very,' Marian said firmly, while navy floral tossed her fiercely permed head.

The large woman, clearly leader of the party, was getting impatient. 'I rather think we're wasting our time,' she said. 'We only popped in to enquire after tipstaves.' Her eyes ranged over the entire stock, lingering over the small assorted items. 'Yes, I rather think we're wasting our time,' she repeated, with a roguish smile.

At this, Paul came forward from his desk at the back of the little shop, managing to look, even in his tight sky-blue trousers with exactly matching shirt, like the owner of a high-class gallery. 'Are you searching for an early tipstave?' he asked in a rich, plummy voice. 'Or for one of the later, ceremonial ones?'

'Any sort. Why? Do you think you could get hold of one for me?' The face she turned towards him was smooth and plump, like the face of a very old child.

'You know, of course, that the later, embellished ones were carried by the Metropolitan police inspectors up until the 1870s,' he said. 'Personally, I think the early specimens are the only ones worth collecting. The others are rather vulgar, in my opinion.'

'Collectable, of course,' Marian added quickly. 'Perhaps the teeniest bit vulgar. But a lot of fun.' (She felt she was getting fluent in antique-speak.)

'I'm going to have the cherub.' Trim, lilac-clad grandmother of Queen's Guide seemed suddenly emboldened. 'Could you pack it very carefully for me, dear? Take care of its little wings, won't you?'

'You have a shrewd eye, Madam,' Paul pronounced. 'I congratulate you.'

The other two women turned away from him as though embarrassed. Marian didn't altogether blame them. She hoped he wouldn't ruin his performance by bowing.

'And I'll take the little duck as well. It would be a shame to leave it behind. I'll have that for myself. For my display cabinet.'

'Well done,' Marian said, when the trio had departed. 'And here was I not realising that you knew your tipstave from your ankle bone.'

'I consulted with Lyle,' Paul said in his normal, slightly Cockney voice, 'as you know perfectly well. Good God, I bet this is a tipstave — one of the early ones, too. Harry Roberts sold it me for a quid. He said it was his grandmother's potato masher. I should have realised it was too well-made for that. I'll have to stand him half a bitter when I see him next.'

I'd really miss this job, Marian thought, if Gerald's right about Paul wanting to sell up and leave. 'What's the trouble?' she asked him, when he was back at his desk again, staring at nothing. 'You don't seem yourself. Are you involved in some particularly shady deal?'

He looked up at her. 'Be innocent of the knowledge, dearest chuck.'

'Macbeth,' she said. An easy guess since that was the play he'd studied for O-level and the only one he'd read.

'My mother wonders if you'd have your coffee upstairs with her this morning.'

'Of course. I'd like to.'

'Sooner rather than later, she says. She had a bad night last night, so she could do with a bit of company.'

'I'll go up as soon as I've finished the dusting...Paul.'

'Yes.'

'You can trust me, you know. It would do you good to talk to someone.'

'I may take you up on that sooner than you think. Various little schemes and stratagem are working to a head. I could need some advice.'

Paul's mother was over eighty and crippled with athritis.

Marian often wondered why she lived with Paul in the small, rather dark flat over the shop. She couldn't be comfortable there. She liked to show off photographs of her other children and grandchildren, their large, posh homes with gardens and swimming pools. Did she think Paul needed her? It was she who had bought him the business, perhaps it was part of the deal that she should live with him; to supervise his life, to stop him getting into trouble.

'Trouble,' she could hear her saying. 'He was trouble even before he was born, dear. I was thirty-eight when I realised he was on the way. My family was complete, Eleanor eleven, Richard ten, Laura eight. You can imagine how awkward it was to have to tell them there was a baby on the way. And when he arrived, he was yellow as a duckling, dear. "Take it away," I said, "it's too hideous, all cock and balls and leering at me. I'd forgotten how nasty babies are." "Please let's keep him, Mummy," Eleanor begged. "I'll look after him. You know how good I've been with the hamsters."'

She talked in a slangy Thirties style. She must once have been considered quite fast, even shocking, Marian thought. Now she was only rather pathetic; large dark eyes and poor gnarled hands.

'I'll go along to Hardiman's and get your Mum some flowers' she said. 'They had some pinks outside, quite cheap. I'll take money from the till, then they can be from both of us.'

'Thanks, love.'

'Those are very pretty, dear. I do miss the garden. It wasn't so bad here when I could get out. I keep telling Paul how lucky he is to have you. Who else would do all his dusting and polishing — not to mention coming up to see his old mother from time to time. Sit down, dear, do.'

The sitting room was faded and shabby, crammed full of furniture; little table, larger table, ornate sideboard, reproduction Dutch dresser, wooden-armed easy chairs — not very easy — vinyl settee, foot-stool, magazine-rack, bureau, yet another table. Where had they all come from, Marian wondered. Were they from Mrs Dainton's previous home in Surrey — perhaps the pieces which had remained unsold at auction — or were they a job-lot, acquired with the shop and flat? The pictures on the wall were bizarre, shiny things with a preponderance of silver and black, there were ornaments every-where; bowls and boxes and vases of glass, china, wood and brass. There seemed nothing that could claim antique value or beauty, yet perhaps Mrs Dainton valued them. Marian hoped so.

'I'm sorry you had a bad night,' she said.

'Who said I had a bad night? He did? Huh! He probably wants you out of the way for some reason. He's expecting a private phone-call, I daresay, or a caller. What does he get up to? I never said anything about a bad night. What a fibber he is. Do you mind getting the coffee, dear? Just instant, unless you'd prefer the other. It makes no dif-ference to me.'

Marian found everything to hand in the tiny kitchen, the tray ready laid and the tin of biscuits nearby.

She looked around her as the kettle came to the boil. Everything clean, every dish washed and in place, the tea-cloth freshly laun-dered and the lino spotless.

'Thank you, dear,' Mrs Dainton said as she returned with the tray. 'I hope it wasn't too much trouble.'

'It was all ready. I did nothing but boil the kettle.'

'He'll make someone a good wife. He had the washing out on the line by eight this morning, he gives me a cooked meal every evening and he'll get the ironing done before he goes out tonight. Now then, what have you got to tell me? Any scandal or gossip?'

Marian described the three women who'd been in the shop earlier, but failed to capture Mrs Dainton's interest. She tried to imitate the whispered asides of the woman in navy, but her hostess spoiled their effect by whole-heartedly agreeing with them all. 'They *are* hideous, those old jelly moulds. And unhygienic. She's right. I wouldn't give them house-room either. People will collect any old rubbish these days. Tipstaves indeed. Chamber-pots, lavatory seats, battered old pots and pans. Madness, if you ask me.'

Marian started to talk about Sally, partly because she couldn't think of anything else, partly because Sally was still very much on her mind.

'And she's young and beautiful with no ties?' Mrs Dainton asked when Marian had finished talking.

'Not young. Heavens no. She's my age.'

'Young,' Mrs Dainton said firmly. 'Young with no ties.'

'She's got one daughter, but she's almost twenty, pretty well off her hands I suppose.'

'She needs to count her blessings. Bring her up here to see me, dear. Why don't you ring her up now and ask her to join us for coffee?'

Mrs Dainton's face lit up at the thought of seeing someone new; someone rather interesting by the sound of things.

'Gerald Maitland is taking her out this morning. He's going to show her the town and the castle.'

'He'll bore her to death. He used to call to see me from time to time but in the end I had to ask him not to. He's more full of useless facts than a foreign encyclopaedia. And that loud, cheerful voice he used to put on. As though I was deaf and senile as well as crippled. Whenever I see him walking down the road now, I shake my fist at him. He likes to pretend I'm joking, but I'm not. Don't you marry him whatever you do.'

'I don't intend to.' (Did she? No, surely not.)

'Good. I wasn't mad about Dr Reed but at least he'd got red blood in his veins.'

Mrs Dainton's dark eyes darted to and fro. As she spoke about Dickie, Marian had the uncomfortable feeling that she was looking for him in the far corner of the room.

'Now your friend Mrs Rushton,' she continued, 'was she fond of Dr Reed?'

'I think so. Why?'

'Don't let her hurt you. I know these greedy, man-eating sort of women, I was one myself. If she tries to suggest that she and Dr Reed...well, if she tries to insinuate anything at all, just smile and shut her up.'

'What an odd idea,' Marian said. 'Dickie had several women friends. He enjoyed flirting, loved nothing better than to have a woman doting on him — nurse or patient or one of my friends — he revelled in it. But he was always so open about it that I was never jealous of anyone, certainly not of Sally. He used to meet her for a

39

drink from time to time when they were both working near Kings Cross, but it was perfectly innocent and above-board.'

'Fore-warned is forearmed,' Mrs Dainton said, as though Marian hadn't spoken. 'I often have premonitions. Somehow I see them together.'

They were silent for a few moments sipping their coffee.

'It's a terrible thing, jealousy,' Mrs Dainton said. 'It tore me to pieces once upon a time. I'd like to be able to help your friend. Would she come to have a cup of tea with me, do you think?'

'Oh dear, perhaps I shouldn't have mentioned her problems. I'm not sure that she'd want everyone to know what she's going through.'

'I'm not everyone, dear. Just a poor old woman that no-one takes notice of.'

Marian studied her. Her small face, usually alive with curiosity, seemed child-like and innocent. If Gerald was right and Paul was thinking of joining his friend in a restaurant in Tenby, what would become of his mother?

'I'll bring her along before the end of the week,' Marian said. 'She'll want to meet you, I know. And now I'm afraid I must get back to the shop. I want to clean the windows before I go home. The sun's made them look so dingy.'

'Has Paul got money troubles, do you think?' Mrs Dainton asked as Marian was about to leave, her over-playing suddenly abandoned.

'I don't know. There's something on his mind.'

'Can't you help him?'

'I'll try. But there's something about me he doesn't trust.'

'Don't let him know I said anything, will you?'

'Of course not.'

Paul seemed himself again when she got back.

'I've sold the elm chest,' he said. 'I let it go for sixty-five. To some Dutch chap. He was thrilled with it.'

Was that what all the anxiety had been about? He'd invited some stranger to visit him in the shop, and wanted her out of the way while he struck up a friendship with him — and sold him an eighteenth century chest for quite a bit less than he'd paid for it.

'It was worth a hundred,' Marian said.

'I know,' he said after a moment's silence. 'Aren't I a fool? And I probably won't see him again. He's only here for a couple of days.'

Marian moved a small tripod table over to the spot in the window where the chest had stood and stepped back to look at it.

'I have to get something out of life,' he said petulantly. 'You try living with her.' He turned his eyes upwards.

'All right. Nobody's getting at you. Being generous isn't a sin.'

'Oh, I'm a damn fool. Now we'll have to over-charge the next customer to get the money back.'

'I'm going to clean the windows,' Marian said. She couldn't pretend to approve of Paul's casual pick-ups. Especially as he had a steady boy-friend whom everyone seemed to like.

FOUR

She's too bloody good to be true, Mrs. Dainton said to herself after Marian left, taking an empty milk bottle downstairs with her. Cosy. Paul's right. Cosy as a feather pillow. Boring as porridge. I bet her friend is much more sparky. I bet she wouldn't waste my time thinking the best of everyone. I wish she was coming to tea on her own. I'd get her talking, see if I wouldn't.

My name should be Malice not Alice, she told herself. The things I've enjoyed most in life have been rows and quarrels and spreading scandal and making mischief. Well, it's amusing. It's entertaining. Why should I sit back and suffer? I suppose I was nice enough once.

She closed her eyes and tried to remember a time when she'd been young and innocent. She couldn't.

No, never, she told herself. My first boyfriend, Charley Watson, I only went out with him because my friend Maisie Bilton fancied him. I only led him on so that I could tell her all about it. 'We've been bad,' I told her, 'and I bet I'll have a baby. Only I couldn't resist him. Oh, he's got such shoulders. When I kissed him I wanted more and more and more.'

I remember how I moved my body to excite her. Why didn't she slap me round the face? It might have cured me. No, she became my slave, begging me for more and more details and offering to try and get me some tablets from her cousin who worked in a Chemists shop in Reigate.

'Then you must get married as soon as possible,' she said, when I told her I didn't want any of her damned pills. 'I'll lend you some money for a dress. I'll come with you to look for rooms.'

I let her arrange a few things for me, even though I knew perfectly well I wasn't up the spout and that I wouldn't marry stupid Charley Watson if I was.

'I've changed my mind,' I told her a few weeks later. 'It's not Charley I'm in love with but his friend, Peter. He's taking me down the park tonight. Why don't you have Charley? He needs comforting. Very cut up he is. No, I'm not having a baby. I found out weeks ago, didn't I tell you?'

And I didn't even like sex, to tell you the truth. All I liked was having a man crazy about me and begging for it. Perhaps I was always something of a man-hater if the truth be known. As well as a woman-hater, I mean.

Of course I got married like everybody else and that was my first big mistake because at that time, 1935, being married was to lose your power. I saw a man catch a salmon once, saw it on the bank, twitching and then still. That's how I felt when I got married.

Robbie the Rat, I called him. He could fight, I give you that, there was nothing soft or sloppy about him. I would probably have enjoyed it except that he had all the bloody weapons.

Especially when I got landed with the baby. And then the next. Two in eighteen bloody months.

Whenever I got violent or vindictive he'd manage to get sent away on business, so that I'd have days and days on my own with no-one to take it out on. And no-one to get the coal in. (That's all a man was expected to do in those days, get the coal in and carve the Sunday joint.)

When I had the third it was even worse. That was the nearest I ever got to turning into a beaten-down housewife, the nearest I ever got to losing my spunk.

It was the war that saved my sanity, the lovely war.

Robbie the Rat was called up the first week — he'd joined the Volunteers in 1938 just to have weekends away from me — and got shipped Overseas in no time at all. He was made an officer, too, so I was getting good money every week with no-one to stop me spending it as I liked. I shared the house with an evacuee family from London, a woman and her two children, and everyone said how bloody marvellous I was because this woman was more than a little bit simple. So simple that she looked after my kids as well as her own, so that I could go out every night with ... who ... well, airmen, soldiers, sailors, Italian prisoners of war when I could, and later on, Yankee soldiers.

What a time. Dances. Cinema. Gin-and-It. Chocolates. Nylons. It was supposed to be a time of scarcity. For me it was a time of plenty.

I was thirty-something by this time and I was the boss, that was the only rule. No sex. Physical feelings limited to hands and lips. I suppose I was pretty cruel — people who've been hurt are always unfeeling — but no-one objected. After all, they were married as well, most of them, so we all kidded ourselves we were being faithful.

'I'm having a grand time,' I wrote to Robbie, 'And I hope you are too. You know I want you to be free and happy like I am.'

Poor sod was in North Africa until 1942.

Every time I dated a lovely new soldier, I thought of the time the Rat had sworn at me because I'd forgotten to get his suit from the cleaners, hadn't had time to iron his white shirt or sew a button on his trousers. And me with three babies on my hands and no help. No washing machine, no biological washing powder, no disposable nappies, no freezer, no instant meals. All the help a woman had in those days was a bottle of gin. It's a wonder we weren't all dipsomaniacs.

'I hope you won't try to escape,' I wrote to him when I heard he was a prisoner-of-war. 'Remember I don't want you shot to pieces.'

To be honest, I didn't want him shot to pieces. I wanted him back so that I could tell him in full detail what a good time I'd been having.

I was — what — thirty-two when the war ended. An American major called Mike Lawson was seriously in love with me at that time — I'd managed to keep relatively free of such complications — and he begged me to divorce Robbie and go to America with him, and I might even have gone except that I found out he was only a small time dairy farmer in civilian life and I didn't see myself as a farmer's wife. Afterwards I often wished I'd thrown my lot in with him and the bleedin' cows.

Not that it wasn't exciting in a way, the Rat's return. The kids painted a Welcome sign and stuck it on our front door, but of course some other local ex-servicemen arrived home first. The kids used to say 'Is this my Dad?' whenever they saw anyone having a cup of tea with me when they came home from school. When at last I said Yes, it was a bit of an anti-climax for them, I think. I don't know that they ever really took to him.

Anyway, we had a few good years when he got back. He thought he was no end of a hero, but I could make him jealous as a baby with no effort at all, just a few reminiscences or even a deep sigh and he was almost whimpering for my attention.

And then the tables were turned again. Christ, Christ, Christ, how stupid and unfair. At the beginning of 1952 he landed a really good job and I got bloody pregnant again.

'What are you muttering about?' Paul asked his mother as he came upstairs from the shop. 'You're talking to yourself far too much. It isn't as though you've had no company this morning. You should try to pull yourself together.'

'Getting pregnant, that's what I was on about. When I was thirty-eight and thought I could look after myself.'

'The Queen was thirty-eight when she had her fourth child. I've just been reading a book about her in the shop.'

'Well, I bet she had a bit more help than I did. And I bet her husband didn't say "Serves you right, you stupid cow," when he found out about it.'

'It didn't give out those sort of details. Only who was her obstetrician and so forth.'

'It rained for a whole week, a whole month perhaps, just after I knew for certain about you. And I cried every day in this bloody pouring rain. That's why you turned out a bloody queer, I think. All that crying damaged you. If I'd shouted and screamed and hurled things about, I might have made a man out of you.'

'What do you want for lunch, sunshine?'

'Nothing. An egg.'

'The Queen eats very lightly when she's eating alone. Even at banquets she specifies very simple dishes. She drinks very little as well. Malvern water or dry white wine. Poached or scrambled?'

'No thanks... Oh, whatever you like.'

'I saw Marian's friend passing the shop this morning with Gerald Maitland,' Paul said from the kitchen. 'Very striking, I must say. Chap I had in the shop said she looked like...'

'She must be round the bend anyway. Good-looks, good health, a well paid job and she can't get over the fact that her husband's thrown her over. What does she need a husband for?'

'But I thought you were the same. Wasn't that the story?'

'The same? I had a sickly baby to look after as well as three other kids.'

'Here's your egg and some nice thin bread and butter.'

'All wanting things. Wanting money, wanting new clothes, wanting bikes, wanting to join the Scouts, the Youth Club, the Brownies. No-one wanting to stay in to look after you so that I could have a night out. Vengeful and furious, that's what I was, not hurt and sloppy like her.'

'Eat it while it's hot.'

'He offered to have Richard. Him and Elspeth. A boy needed a father, he said. "What about the baby?" I shrieked at him. "He's a boy as well, or haven't you noticed? Both boys or neither." Of course it turned out to be neither. Nobody'd have taken you. Nobody in their right mind. Little yellow monkey, you were. Ugly little frog.'

'For God sake, eat your egg. It's just as you like it.'

'Do you remember Elspeth?' she asked him.

'Of course I do.'

'A real lady she was. Very soft-voiced and mild. The worst type. Of course I had my own back on her. But that wasn't until four or five years later. At the beginning I had to be content with poisoning the children's minds and getting them to spy on her.'

'Cream crackers and Brie? It's a bit runny, needs to be eaten.'

Realising that Paul had stopped listening to her reminiscences she carried on talking to herself. It was almost as good. 'A large woman she was, wide and solid rather than plump, with a large, composed face and large, straight legs.'

'Coffee or tea?'

'Yes please. She'd have made a handsome man, she looked a bit like Anthony Eden. Enormous feet, size seven or eight I should think. I wrote her an anonymous letter once. I remember getting cheap lined paper and putting a doughnut on it to get the right,greasy effect. Straggly illiterate capital letters. YOR MAN IS AVIN IT ORFF WITH A FITTEEN YR OLD AND THE PLICE IS INTRESSTED TOOTSEY. Just a jokey letter, nothing vicious. But, do you know what, she returned it to me unopened, simply put the greasy envelope into a clean one and re-addressed it to me. Complacent cow.'

'Yes, I think I'll have a nap now. Just draw the curtains, will you. Are you going out tonight? Meeting Gareth?'

'Yes, I'll probably be going out. But I may just go to the Farmers. Some interesting people staying there this week.'

'I think I'll have my eiderdown, dear. Yes I know it's warm, but it helps me get to sleep.'

'Of course when the Rat next came — he used to bring money every Friday and call again on the Sunday to take the kids out, only Eleanor was refusing to go with him at that time if I remember right — anyway when he came, I couldn't resist showing him the letter. It was such a little masterpiece, I wanted someone to see it. Well, you should have seen him trying to keep his face straight. And the very next time he came he brought me a bottle of gin. I think he was touched because I'd signed it Tootsey which was what his mother used to call his thing when he was small. Anyway, that was the first time the ice cracked between us.'

Paul washed up and then got ready to go back to the shop.

'I'm off now, Mum. I've got some paperwork to do this afternoon. Marian isn't coming in. You'll be all right?'

She closed her eyes to avoid having to answer him.

'God, but you were small,' she said after he'd gone. 'Small and sickly. The others had been fat and pink and greedy like their father. You were like a half-dead rabbit. That's why I loved you most, I suppose. I've always been a contrary bitch.'

Of course I remember the fat cow, Paul said to himself as he went downstairs. Aunt Elspeth. How could anyone forget her? That time they took me on holiday with them for instance. When Dad kept telling me how lucky I was, for God's sake, and how well I'd got to behave, eat nicely with my mouth closed and please and thank you every time she as much as looked at me.

I'd never stayed at a hotel before.

I liked the lifts, but I wasn't allowed to go in them on my own. I wasn't allowed to do anything except walk about with them and play on the bleedin' sands and not with other children because they might not be suitable. We didn't go to the pictures or to any of the seaside shows because we'd miss our dinner which had been paid for and waste not want not. She used to talk in French when she wanted to say something about my mother which sounded much worse than silly old bitch which was what my mother said about her.

Christ, so many long dreary meals in that big dining room that always smelled of yesterday's gravy and so many long boring walks by the sea. 'This will have to last you till next year, old chap,' my father said on the last evening, 'make the most of it.' And then she said in a voice she might have thought I couldn't hear but didn't care much if I did, 'Oh, I never said he could come with us *every* year.' And I was thinking, I'd rather be burned on a fire than come with you again, you boring old cow.

And that's what I told my mother when I got back. And of course she shrieked with delight and hugged me and promised to take me to a funfair before I went back to school.

I don't think she did though.

FIVE

When Marian went home to lunch she found Sally reading in the garden.

'You look a lot better,' she said, 'and happier. What are you reading?'

'A book Gerald lent me. Legends and Folk Tales. It's about this area. It's interesting.'

'I was afraid you'd still be out with him.'

'He offered me lunch but I decided I'd rather come back here. I suppose I wanted a rest from him.'

'What did you do? I expected you to drop in on us.'

We looked for you but you weren't in the shop when we passed. We saw Paul, but he was busy with someone. I must say, he doesn't look gay. God, I can't stand gays. How can you bear to work for him?'

'I like him. He's fun. You'd like him too.'

'Gerald doesn't seem over-keen on him.'

'I dare say he'll survive that. Did you like the town? Where did you go?'

'We had coffee in the Castle and then we walked as far as the bridge and out on to the main road. Yes, it's a nice town. It's real somehow. The food shops are real — do you know what I mean? They have good food, it smells of food, but they don't feel the need to turn everything out into little wicker baskets as though they're playing at shops. They're real. The people seem real too.'

'Good,' Marian said, trying to sound mildly discouraging — she wasn't fond of Sally's lapses into metaphysics — but not downright rude, 'I'm glad you approve.'

'Shall we have lunch out here?' Sally asked. 'The weather is so lovely.'

'Yes, let's. I often do when it's fine. And I'm not going back to the shop this afternoon, so we can take our time.'

'Shall I help?'

Sally suddenly managed to look and sound exhausted.

'No, I'll manage. There's nothing much to do.'

In the kitchen, chopping chives and basil for the salad dressing, Marian was annoyed with herself for having refused Sally's offer of help. If she wasn't careful she'd find herself in the same subservient position as when they'd shared a flat in the third year at University; Martha to Sally's Mary, she doing the shopping and getting the meals and Sally doing the flowers and entertaining the guests — usually hers.

'I've picked some flowers,' Sally said at the door. 'I just want to look for a container. I don't want a vase, I want something shaped like this.'

She spread out her hands in front of her, looking for a moment like a Victorian statuette.

'This will do,' she said.

She ran water into the small blue and white tureen Marian was going to use for the tomatoes and took it out with her.

Flowers on the table, Marian thought. Now I suppose I'll have to find a white cloth and decent glasses.

She remembered a holiday in the South of France they'd once had together; she and Sally, Alan and Dickie and the three children. They'd stayed in some primitive farmhouse, the weather had been perfect, they'd drunk a lot of wine and eaten simple meals; delicious cooked meats and paté from the charcuterie in the village, local-grown vegetables and salads, and fish from the nearby harbour town. She'd had a wonderful holiday that year, because Dickie had insisted on making a rota so that every task was equally divided. She remembered afternoons when she'd been able to lie in the sun, blissfully idle, knowing that it was Alan's turn to supervise the children on the beach while Sally and Dickie were in charge of the evening meal; shopping as well as all the preparation. She'd have to suggest rotas if Sally intended to stay for any length of time.

Not that everything had been altogether straightforward even on that holiday. One day, when it was Dickie and Sally's turn to go shopping in town, they'd been persuaded by a local fisherman to go out with him to fish for their supper, he'd got into some difficulty with the boat and had had to pull in on to an island a couple of miles out to get something or other seen to, and they weren't back until about nine or ten o'clock.

Alan had refused to let her worry. 'Listen to me, they're perfectly safe,' he'd said, 'They're in some bar or other enjoying themselves. I know Sally, she's got no sense of time.' He and she had taken the children out to the café-restaurant in the village which looked dreadful — little tables covered with oil-cloth and a cat on the counter — but where they'd had a wonderful meal, and by the time they'd arrived back at the house the other two were there.

She carried out white cloth, decent glasses and cutlery.

'Do you remember that holiday we had in the South of France?' she asked Sally. 'Do you remember the day you and Dickie went out fishing with one of the local fishermen and didn't get back till dark?'

It was some time before Sally answered. 'Why bring that up now?' she said at last. 'You must know perfectly well that there wasn't any fisherman. Dickie insisted on taking me out in a boat, he rowed to the island and we stayed there too long.'

Marian was both surprised and shocked. 'Why ever did you invent that other story then?'

'Because Alan would have been furious with us.'

They ate in silence for a while. Marian couldn't help thinking about Mrs Dainton's strange fancy, 'I see them together,' but after a few moments was able to dismiss it. Perhaps Dickie and Sally had had a brief holiday flirtation but it was certainly no more because Dickie had steadfastly refused to contemplate another holiday with them. That didn't seem like any great romance.

It was Sally who broke the silence. 'Gerald is really very knowledgeable about this area, isn't he? I didn't expect to be as impressed by him as I was.'

'Yes. I remember Dickie saying that someone in the grip of an obsession was always interesting, and Gerald is certainly that. He thinks he knows more about the Preseli mountains than God. Not that he believes in God anyway.'

'Why, do you?' Sally was as surprised as though Marian had admitted to a belief in witchcraft or flying saucers.

'I suppose I do in a way,' Marian said. 'Nothing very definite. I don't go to church these days. But yes, I suppose I do have some sort of belief. It's here in my blood stream even if not in my brain. When poor Dickie died I remember feeling...'

Sally interrupted her. 'Gerald believes in some sort of Earth Magic,' she said. 'He believes that an energy emanates from the standing stones and the burial mounds and that this can effect us if we let it.'

Marian looked at her to see whether she was being serious. She was.

'Well, my mother used to believe something rather similar about churches,' she said, rallying herself, 'old churches and cathedrals. She'd often go and sit in a church and feel that some sort of grace had descended on her. I suppose I feel much the same about the natural world, trees and hills and so on. I mean, you can feel restored in a way, can't you? I mean by the something, something far more deeply interfused, whose dwelling is the light of setting suns and the round ocean and the living air. You know what I mean.'

Sally, unable to wait any longer for Marian to notice that her glass was empty, reached for the bottle and poured herself more wine. 'As I understand it,' she said, 'Gerald believes in something far more definite than a vague spiritual glow.'

'Does he? I'm afraid I usually shut him up when he starts on his "Standing stones, dolmens, burial grounds, stone circles, round and long barrows." That was the title of one of his talks to the Tenby and District History Society. Tim used to recite it like a lift attendant whenever he came to call.'

'You're changing the subject,' Sally said. 'You're always doing that. We were talking about the possibility of picking up energy waves from...'

'It sounds adolescent to me.'

'You're alarmed by the idea.'

'Oh, don't be absurd. I've been to several of the sites and felt absolutely nothing.'

'He's taking me to one of the burial mounds tomorrow.'

Lucky old you, Marian thought, but refrained from saying anything.

They lapsed into another silence.

'These white roses are so beautiful,' Sally said then, taking one from the arrangement in the tureen and cradling it as though it were a wounded bird. 'What are they called?'

'They're a damask rose. Madame Hardy, I think.' Marian bent to smell them. 'Dickie was mad about old roses. He had a garden-full in Ealing,'

'I remember,' Sally said dreamily, while Marian tried not to notice the way she was suddenly plucking the petals from the rose she held in her hand.

'I remember we'd been to a party out your way, and we called on our way home. It was long past midnight but Dickie insisted on taking me to see them by torch-light.'

'Yes. However late he came home, he'd always go out to see them and smell them.'

Sally helped herself to more wine. 'Odd really,' she said. 'He wasn't the type of man you'd associate with gardens and flowers was he?'

Marian sat back to consider the question, but Sally answered for her.

'No. Fast cars, expensive restaurants, beautiful clothes. He always wore very elegant suits.'

'Yes. But his leisure clothes were a bit of a joke, weren't they? He used to work so hard at looking casual.'

Sally looked at her with surprise. 'I think that's the first unkind thing I've ever heard you say about Dickie,' she said.

'Well, it's a healthy sign, I suppose. I try not to idealize him too much. He was a strange mixture.'

'I suppose so. This town, for instance, isn't the sort of place I'd have expected him to choose for a holiday cottage. He was more the type for one of those trendy little yachting places on the South Coast. Or did you choose this place?'

'No, he did. I was rather surprised by it, too.'

Marian didn't intend to say anymore, but Sally was looking at her intently, willing her to continue.

'You see, he used to come here on holiday when he was a boy. And he used to say they were his only happy times. He didn't have an easy childhood, he was an only child and his parents fought a lot, but they were always happy when they were here. So he was determined to come back to live here when he was grown-up. This holiday cottage was only the first step. He wanted a practice down here. He wanted to buy that big white house on the hill. He'd probably have got it, too, if he'd lived.'

'He'd never have come to live here,' Sally said.

'I don't know. He loved the place. He had two sides, Sally, one very practical and down-to-earth and one very emotional, even sentimental.'

Sally was quiet and seemed withdrawn, but all the same Marian had the feeling that she was listening with interest and attention.

'He tried hard to hide his sentimental side. When friends used to say how foolish it was to buy a week-end cottage so far from London, he'd point out how much cheaper property was in Pembrokeshire. He'd never admit that he'd had to come back here.'

'Had to? Surely that's putting it a bit strongly?' Sally's voice seemed unnecessarily sharp.

'Perhaps,' Marian answered quietly. 'It certainly seemed like a compulsion to me.'

Marian remembered, as she pulled at the short grass underneath her dangling hand, the heat of the afternoon and the heavy scents of the little garden lapping round her, their first visit to the tumble-down cottage in the small grey town.

'It's boring,' nine-year-old Johnny had decided. 'What can we do here? Away from all our friends. There's hardly any garden. Where can we ride our bikes? Where can we play football? It's dead boring.'

'I'll make you a swing from that tree,' Dickie had replied. 'We'll play ludo and snakes-and-ladders in the evenings. We'll read round the table and be a happy family.' John and Tim had looked at him pityingly.

'The sea's very near,' she'd added. 'Don't forget the sea.'

'Oh yes, the sea,' Dickie had assented, rather grudgingly. In his childhood, going to the sea had been a rare occurence. It was the hills which had drawn him back.

'I always knew I'd come back here,' he'd told her later that night when they were in the Castle Hotel getting ready for bed.

It was then he'd told her about Ann Hopkins, the landlady at the boarding house where they always stayed. She was a simple, child-less country woman, whose husband had been killed in Normandy during the war, and who made her living keeping visitors. She was plump and kind and motherly, everything his own mother was not. She had a great affection for Dickie and would often take him out in between washing up after lunch and preparing the evening meal.

One day she'd taken him to visit her grandmother who lived in the mountains, five miles away. The old woman had felt his head, held his hands, looked into his eyes as though mesmerised, and said that his destiny lay with them. He'd come back, she'd said, and be a doctor or a member of parliament or some other great man.

'Was she a witch?' she'd asked, ashamed of the question as soon as it was spoken and expecting to be ridiculed for it.

'Ann simply said a wise woman,' he'd said softly. 'She said she knew different things from other people because she'd never been to school, never leant to read. I certainly thought she was a witch. She looked so old and fierce, and my skin where she touched me, tingled with cold. I could feel her touch for hours. I was very alarmed by her.'

'Mrs Hopkins shouldn't have taken you to see her. She only said you'd come back because she knew that was what you wanted to hear.'

'I suppose so. Only, you know, this is a very strange area, very wild and primitive.'

'Nonsense,' she'd said comfortingly. The double bed at the Castle was soft and warm and his arm was around her.

'I suppose it is, if you say so,' he'd said. 'So what made me pay far too much for that pile of old stones up the road?'

She couldn't help wondering the same thing.

It was about three months later that they'd come down for their annual summer holiday.

In their absence the builders had been at work. The roof had been re-tiled, the kitchen and bathroom re-built, the other rooms re-decorated, and with much of the heavy old furniture left by the previous owners removed, it had seemed a different place.

Dickie had taken the boys out to explore the town while she'd unpacked and hung up the pretty floral curtains she'd been making. She'd felt surprisingly contented, she remembered, wondering how she could have been so disappointed and dispirited on her last visit.

'We've bought a china dog and a patchwork tea-cosy,' Dickie'd said, when he and the boys had come back. 'There's a junk shop down by the bridge.'

'And Dad got us a game called bagatelle,' John had said. 'It's ace. He used to play it when he was little and he showed us how. I beat Tim hollow.'

'Anyway, I can't play when I'm hungry,' Tim had said. 'And anyway, it's only a game, anyway.'

'I've never been so happy,' Dickie had said, kissing her.

'I was thinking about Dickie,' she told Sally when she looked up and saw her staring at her.

'So was I,' Sally said. 'I was wondering why he'd never wanted to come on another holiday with us. We had such a good time in Provençe.'

'He loved being here,' Marian said, 'that's why. He used to say this was the only place he was ever really happy.'

The silence of early afternoon settled on them. The only noise to be heard was the whirr of an electric saw in the distance, and nearer at hand, a thrush cracking a snail on a stone. Why didn't the rain come? So many hot, close days. The roses were dropping their petals before they'd properly opened. The mournful hills seemed to be moving closer, menacing the town.

SIX

The earth,' Gerald was saying. 'Feel it. Put your hands on it. Don't you feel its force, its energy?'

Sally closed her eyes. She was sitting on the short cropped grass, both hands pressed onto the ground behind her.

Above her, a lark ascended, its astonishing crescendo breaking her concentration. 'A lark,' she said, recognising it from Vaughan Williams. Gerald grunted.

They'd just finished a delicious picnic lunch, thick slices of slightly pink beef, chicken vol-au-vent, salad, French bread, fruit, cheese and a bottle of Côtes du Rousillion. Gerald prided himself on his picnics and was always appalled by Marian who insisted that she was perfectly happy with raspberry jam sandwiches and tea from a flask.

The lark descended, its free fall broken only a few feet from the ground.

'I've been out of touch too long,' Sally said at last.

There was certainly a throb of sound; when the larks were quiet for a moment, the bees and grasshoppers filled the silence like some distant engine. Was that what Gerald meant?

'No-one is out of touch,' he said.

'Nor can foot feel being shod,' Sally quoted. Though, in fact, she had slipped off her sandals an hour or so before.

'The earth has powers to heal,' Gerald insisted. 'Feel its pulse.'

Sally stood up, planting her bare feet firmly on its warm surface. Her short, almond-green dress showed off her bare brown legs.

'This hill has been sacred for thousands of years,' Gerald said. 'Look at the stones up there. That's where they gathered for their religious festivals, their high days and holy days.'

'What sort of people were they?' Sally asked. In such a wild, remote place it was impossible not to feel a hint of their presence.

'They worked hard. They were in touch with the earth. They tried to live at peace.'

'They'd all choose our lives, given half a chance. Central heating and the telly.'

Gerald refused to be deflected. 'We sleep our lives away. Swinish slumber. All our labour-saving devices giving us so much leisure. And what do we do with our leisure? Fritter it away on mindless pastimes. Pass-times. Pursuits to make time pass. That's what we've come to. We endeavour to make time pass, when we should be using it purposefully and mourning its passing. Living.'

'But what do you mean by living? I've felt alive from time to time, really alive. I've been happy from time to time, excited very often. Isn't that living?'

He looked at her, then beyond her. 'I planned to build a wooden shelter, a small round hut just there, or perhaps over by that crag on the horizon, planned to stay here for a whole year, rising at dawn, searching for wood and turf for my fire, gathering food, sowing and reaping, getting to grips with the climate, getting to know the mysteries of the land, the habits of the wild animals and birds.'

'So why don't you?' Sally asked with a burst of impatience. It didn't seem a very difficult project. Other people crossed oceans single-handed.

'Too old,' he said. And looked old as he spoke.

'So why didn't you do it when you could?'

'I always had too much work. My career was always at stake. I always had to keep one jump ahead of someone or other.' The wavering look in his eyes upset Sally. She didn't want to start feeling sorry for him; it was against her instincts.

'You could still spend the summer months here. You could still spend a year here if you had a companion. Surely a young student would jump at the chance of a year with you. He could do the bulk of the hard work, and keep a journal which could form the basis of a thesis.'

'It's too late. I've wasted my life. Used up my energies on all manner of unimportant schemes and unimportant people. Worked for promotion, only because I wanted to prove my superiority, and when I was promoted, became an administrator. Of course, I told myself I could do my real work in my spare time, but there seemed less and less of it. And when I eventually retired, I became a television personality, trotting out glib theories to audiences who only want glib theories.'

'But you must get pleasure from it? Satisfaction? To know that you're becoming a household name?'

'Vanity. The last vice we lose.'

'You think you'd be happier if you'd remained an obscure scholar?

57

That would have made you feel more real?'

'I'm sure of it. A man with a job of work to do. I've barely time now to accomplish anything. But I must get my book written. I have to vindicate myself to that extent.'

He turned to Sally. 'And what will you do now?' he asked her, conscious of having talked too much about himself. 'You don't seem the type who's going to waste any part of her life. I know you've had a nasty shock recently, but you'll very soon get over it, I know that, too. And what then?'

But Sally wasn't interested in discussing failure, disappointment and frustrated ambition, either Gerald's or her own. She'd come out with him to see pre-historic sites, to gain something from them. That's what he'd promised her. He'd told her they were places where energy was concentrated, an energy which couldn't be destroyed. He'd even suggested that the small chambers inside the tombs could have been intended for those seeking mystic experiences. Yet now that they were so near, he seemed reluctant to let her test his theories. Perhaps he wasn't as confident about them as he pretended to be.

'Shall we walk further up the mountain?' she asked. 'I'd like to see what remains of that burial mound you were talking about.'

'Let's wait till it's cooler,' he said. 'We're all right where we are. This is all holy ground.'

Sally turned on him. 'Are you serious when you say things like that? Holy ground? Do you really believe the theories you told me about? Do you really believe that these people were able to make use of an energy that we know nothing about?'

'They could solve complicated mathematical problems. They had a formidable knowledge of astronomy. They could easily have had other kinds of knowledge, a knowledge of the earth's power which is buried with them.'

'A form of magic?' Sally wanted a definite commitment from Gerald, but he wouldn't be pinned down. She saw him weighing her words in his mind. What did he believe?

He suddenly sat up straighter. 'I brought my wife here once,' he said.

Sally tried not to look surprised or especially interested. Marian had told her that Gerald never mentioned his wife, wouldn't even answer questions about her. She waited, her eyes on the ground, for him to continue.

'And not long before her death,' he said. 'It was a lovely spring day, one of those benevolent April days that are warm as summer.'

She waited again for him to continue, waited several moments.

'What happened?' she asked at last.

'Nothing much,' he said. 'But it's a day I like to remember.'

He sighed and looked at his hands. He rubbed the brown spots on them as though he could rub them away.

When he spoke next it was in a different voice. 'Won't you tell me why you're so unhappy?' he asked. 'It's not really because your husband left you, is it?'

'Why do you say that?'

'There's something much deeper and more secret, it seems to me. More intense. Something you feel guilty about? Am I right?'

'Doesn't everyone feel guilty about almost everything?' Sally said crossly. 'I'd like to go back now, Gerald. We've been here hours.'

'Dickie. You had an affair with Dickie?'

'Gerald. I can't see that any affairs I may have had are any concern of yours.'

Gerald didn't answer for a moment. 'Except that I'd like to help you,' he said at last. 'All our great tormenting secrets are such paltry things, aren't they, in a place like this? Don't you feel that?'

'I feel calmer than I did,' she admitted. 'But that's all I'm going to say.'

'I'm sorry I mentioned poor Dickie. I knew he'd been something of a philanderer in the past, that's all. He never admitted as much, of course, but I recognised the signs. Set a thief to catch a thief. You know what I mean.'

Sally had decided that she wasn't going to have much help from poor old Gerald. Marian had been right. The power he pretended to feel was nothing but some form of self-induced hysteria.

As soon as she said she wanted to leave, though, Gerald was eager to take her to see the burial chamber.

She declined his offer.

'I can't understand your obsession with this place,' she said. 'What's so special about it? There are pre-historic sites all over Europe, all over the world. Far more impressive ones than these.'

'These are the sites I've studied.'

'So? I should have thought you'd be all the more bored by them by this time.'

Gerald seemed to shrink at her words. For a time he occupied himself with the picnic things, salvaging some of the remains, disposing of others, closing plastic containers, putting everything back in its rightful place in the basket. What an old granny he was, Sally thought. What a useless old granny.

'Some years ago, I suppose you could say I was near to getting bored,' he said. 'But then I was caught up, yes, captivated by certain old myths which seem to belong to this area rather than to any other. In a sense, they gave life to old stones.'

'The myths and legends you gave me to read?'

'The book I gave you was a simplified version of them. If you like, I'll lend you the book which moved me so much. It's not a very old book. The legends weren't commited to writing until the thirteenth century and they contain quite recent material about the Romans and about Arthur and his court, but they also contain remnants of myths which were handed down from generation to generation from these times.'

He was looking up at the crest of the hill as he spoke.

'These times,' Sally repeated, for the first time feeling a tightening in her throat, feeling something of the brooding intensity of the landscape.

'These times. The time of the Matriarchal society, the time of the Queen Goddess. There are definite glimpses of that era in the work, as well as traces — almost obscured, of course, because they meant little to the thirteenth century writer — of the male's later struggle to overcome the power of the female.'

Sally was looking at him intently now. 'Go on,' she said.

'Rhiannon, whose singing birds had the power to assuage sorrow, was one of the Great Mothers, probably corresponding to Rhea, the virgin mother of Zeus in Greek mythology. She's become degenerated to a mortal woman in certain sections of the book, but in others, her deity is still distinctly recognisable. And Lleu's mother, Arianrhod, was another Goddess. She was so afraid that her son would usurp her power that she put a spell on him, that he should never have name, arms or a wife. But Gwydion, the magician, archetypal patriarch, tricked Lleu's mother into giving him name and arms and later he created for him a woman out of wild flowers. "Gwydion, son of Dôn of mighty powers, Who made by magic a woman from flowers." The words are by Taliesin, a sixth century poet, but he's re-telling stories which go back to pre-historic times.'

60

'And these sites are from those matriarchal times?'

'Undoubtedly. Yes, it was the Goddess who was worshipped here, the Queen-Goddess who led the tribe, with the king, simply a consort, replaced when necessary. In fact, it's still the religion that comes most naturally to us in Britain. That's why the Puritans had to clamp down on the Virgin-worship in Christianity. It was rapidly reverting to the old religion with all its pagan rites.'

'Paganism makes more sense of the world,' Sally said.

Gerald nodded his agreement. 'More sense than the decadent form of patriarchal religion we're left with now,' he said, 'with Father Christmas its most potent symbol. At least paganism contains joy as well as sorrow and cruelty. The Goddess does give herself to man, even if the price is high.'

Gerald sank back into a contemplation of his many love affairs, seeking some comfort, but only succeeding in sinking deeper into sadness and remorse.

But Sally's star had risen as his had sunk. She'd caught the sun. She was suddenly full of energy, savage in her beauty, her cheeks the bronzed pink of young oak leaves. To her surprise she saw that the grass around her hand was full of tiny flowers and minute insects.

She leaned towards Gerald, her weight on her strong, round arms; her eyes drew him towards her.

'It's time to go,' he said, getting to his feet. 'Marian will be wondering where we are.'

After they had gone, the cloudless blue sky gradually paled. A light wind blew up and the short grass whispered and stirred. Owls and other night-birds screeched, a fox barked, a stoat screamed. On the mountains, the whole of time was only a day and a night.

SEVEN

This is Sally, Mrs Dainton, my friend Sally Rushton.'
What a clever woman, Mrs Dainton thought. She seems to smell of love and intrigue, can it be only her perfume? Her clothes seem a part of her. What's that word, sensuous, that's it.

'I hope you'll excuse me staring at you, my dear,' she said. 'I don't get to see many new faces these days. I'm pleased to meet you, I'm sure.'

Was my skin ever as pink and flawless as hers, she wondered. No, I was never a beauty. Well, perhaps I was lucky. Her sort of looks must take a lot of organising, I had time to think of other things.

'This is a lovely room,' Sally said, in what Marian thought of as her throbbing voice. 'The hills in the distance. They must be such a comfort to you.' She walked through the maze of furniture to the window.

'They are,' Mrs Dainton said soulfully. 'I will lift up mine eyes unto the hills from whence cometh my help.'

Marian shot her a quick glance. 'For goodness' sake,' she said, 'Let's not get morbid. Shall I put the kettle on?'

'Magic hills,' Sally said, turning towards them again. 'The hills of Rhiannon. Do you know the stories, Mrs Dainton?'

'No, I don't, dear. I'm not Welsh, you see. We've only been here the last thirteen years. Now Paul's friend is Welsh. He'd probably know all those tales. He speaks Welsh, he does. They speak Welsh in the north of Pembrokeshire, but not in this part, I'm sure I don't know why.'

'It's because the Flemings settled in the South of Pembrokeshire in the fourteenth century. They're a different people,' Sally said.

'You've been listening to Gerald Maitland, haven't you dear? He tried to lend me books about these parts once, but I couldn't get into them. To tell you the truth, I don't like fairy stories. If I read a book, I like it to be about ordinary people like you and me. With something a bit sinister in the background. *Riches* is the best book I've read for a long time. I like a book to have plenty of action in it. When I was young, there was only dots.'

'I thought *Riches* was rather over-done, though. Larger than life, I thought.'

'Larger than life,' Marian said, coming back from the kitchen with a tray. 'I should have thought a woman on a pale white steed appearing out of nowhere was slightly larger than life as well.'

'But she was a Goddess,' Sally said, 'come to choose a mortal man to give her a child. There were no Gods, you see, only Goddesses.'

She spoke levelly and patiently like someone explaining the life-cycle of the common frog.

'Fancy.' Mrs Dainton said, meeting Marian's eyes.

'Goddess,' Sally continued. 'It makes me angry that we only have words like Goddess and Priestess, words which indicate a diminution, a reduction. We should have something different and larger and essentially female.'

'Thank goodness for witch,' Marian said, 'and of course trollop. Will you have a scone, Mrs Dainton?' she continued rapidly, before Sally could come in with a retort of any sort. 'Paul had got everything ready, fair play to him. Blackcurrant jelly? Oh, don't let's get intense and intellectual. It's too hot. I rather like fairy stories myself, but I just accept them for what they are — meaningless fantasies.'

'I really can't eat anything,' Sally said, spooning jam on to her buttered scone and devouring it in two gulps. How did she keep so slim, Marian wondered, when she ate like a teenager, finishing off things like potato salad and lemon meringue pie without seeming to know she was doing it.

'If they're meaningless fantasies,' Sally said, when her mouth was empty, 'how do you account for the fact that the same themes occur in the mythologies of all nations? The myth of Persephone for instance, whose abduction causes winter in the land?'

'It's because of the television,' Mrs Dainton answered. 'Satellites, and that.'

'Did Paul tell you that he sold another Persian rug this morning?' Marian asked Mrs Dainton in a loud, firm voice. 'The one I took home to wash — I brought it up to show you last week. Paul was sure I'd ruin it, but it brought out the colours beautifully. I washed it in the bath, with rain water and baby soap and dried it on the orchard wall.'

'And how much did you get for it, after all that?' Mrs Dainton asked.

'Ninety-five pounds, which wasn't a bad price since Paul had bought it in an auction with four others. I'm surprised no-one else noticed them. He got the lot for thirty pounds. I'm getting really interested in Oriental rugs. I'm going to try and get a book about them in London tomorrow.'

'Going to London tomorrow?' Mrs Dainton said.'That's nice, dear. Both of you?'

'Not me. I've just come from there,' Sally said, another scone poised in her hand.

'No, I'm going on my own. It's a business trip.'

'On a Saturday? Funny day for a business trip. Oh, excuse me, dear. I'm being nosey again.'

'Well, I'm...Well, it's something I'd rather not talk about at the moment. You know how it is. In case nothing comes of it.'

'Are you thinking of moving back to London, dear? I'm always telling Paul that you will. There's no-one for her here. I've said that time and time again. Who will she meet in this place? What is there for her here? Back in London, she'll have all her posh friends inviting her round to dinner-parties and she'll get a new husband in no time.'

'I'm not going back to London, Mrs Dainton, whatever you may have told Paul. And I'm not actually on the look-out for a new husband, either.'

'Well, whether you are or not, there's no-one for you here. When the new vicar came, the first thing I wanted to know was, married or single. Married with three children. Everyone's married round here. And the divorce rate is very low, that's another thing I've noticed. And all the unmarried men are queer.'

'A thing Jane Austen didn't take into account,' Sally said.

'And another thing is that women don't die in childbirth any more. Marian would make a very suitable step-mother,' she told Sally, 'being so good-natured. Well, she's too good-natured. Fancy taking one of those filthy old rugs home and washing it in her bath. Goodness knows where it had been. Who else would do a thing like that? And she's not appreciated, not here. You surely don't think Paul appreciates it? No, what you want is a widower, thirty-five to forty, with two or three young children to bring up.'

'Why don't you advertise?' Sally said, rousing herself. 'A middle-aged woman...'

'A doctor's widow,' Mrs Dainton said. 'Never mind middle-aged. 'An attractive doctor's widow, own children grown, would like to meet a something, something widower or divorcee, view matrimony.'

'View long-term relationship,' Sally said.

'What about the something, something?' Marian asked, deciding that this topic of conversation was less fraught than many others. 'What are the basic requirements? Handsome? Good-tempered? Well-educated?'

'Exciting,' Mrs Dainton said. 'Excitement is the only thing. If you have a red-blooded man you don't have to waste time dreaming. My husband was a dirty rotter, but at least he was red-blooded. Young, that's another thing you want. You don't want a dry old stick like Gerald Maitland.'

'I think Gerald Maitland is rather nice,' Marian said.

'And you don't want anyone that's rather nice either. Rich, young, exciting. You,' she said to Sally, 'could take your pick.'

But Sally had got up and was again looking out at the hills, now bathed in a faint coppery light. She felt she was looking at the back-drop of a theatre. There was an urgent sense of something about to happen. 'The weather's breaking,' she said, 'Look at the clouds rushing at the mountains. And now, look how dark it's getting. No wonder our ancestors believed in Gods and Goddesses. We were taking steps to plan our own destiny, and look how angry they are. There'll be thunder and lightning any moment now.'

'You'd think she really believes in all that,' Mrs Dainton said, tipping her head towards Sally, who was still standing at the window.

'She's not very well,' Marian mouthed.

'I know what you mean,' Mrs Dainton said. A beautiful woman, she thought, but mad as old Hetty Lewis in her trilby. 'Who's looking after her...I mean, who's keeping her company tomorrow? When you go to London?'

'She says she'll take my place in the shop in the morning.'

'Really! Perhaps she'll come and have a cup of coffee with me?'

'I'm sure she'd like to, but I doubt if she'll have the time, Mrs Dainton. You see, Paul's got to be out as well.'

'Paul? What's he got to be out for? There's no sales on a Saturday.'

'One or two things he's got to do, it seems.'

'In other words, you don't want to tell me.'

'I'm not in his confidence, Mrs Dainton. I don't question him.'

'I question him enough, but I don't get any answers. Is it about her,' (another nod towards Sally who was still at the window) 'that you're going to London?'

'Sort of. I really can't say more at the moment.'

'I quite understand, dear.' She leaned over and patted Marian's hand.

'We'd better get home before the rain comes,' Marian said.

Sally turned from the window. 'And after the mist, lo every place filled with light,' she said in a low voice.

It became even darker after Marian and Sally had left, but the expected rain still held off. Slowly and laboriously, Mrs Dainton got herself up and then shuffled across the room, to sit at the small window overlooking the street.

The exercise proved worthwhile. The young woman in the flat across the road had turned her light on; she could see her staring at herself in a mirror, trying on different pairs of earrings, holding her cigarette at different angles and blowing smoke at her reflection. She seemed to be in her petticoat. Or was it a sun-dress? Earlier in the year she'd had a job as a lollipop-lady at the Infants School, but it hadn't lasted long. She probably couldn't get up in time. Her husband worked in the television shop down the road. When he came home she became more sulky and bored-looking than ever. She'd once seen them having a fight.

She'd often asked Paul to invite them over for a drink, but he wouldn't. They weren't her type, he said; he was football-mad and she was always in the Farmers playing darts with anyone who'd buy her a drink. How did he know what her type was? He didn't even know their names. She thought the young man, stocky and neat in his navy-blue overalls, was probably a Dave or a Steve, but she couldn't decide about the broad-faced, broad-hipped young woman. In some lights she looked a Eunice. She had a daughter-in-law called Eunice who was always good for a fight.

It was strange how names affected the personality. Peggy was a very dependable sort of a name. What were they having for supper, she wondered. One of those instant meals, she wouldn't mind betting.

Oh to be young, she thought, to scowl all day, to plonk down a foil carton of braised beef in gravy in front of one's husband, to spend an evening playing darts in a pub.

'For God's sake don't leave that Sally woman in the shop on her own.

66

I don't understand why Marian didn't warn you. She's mad.'

Paul Dainton took away his mother's breakfast tray, sighing as he did so. 'You've got it wrong as usual,' he said. 'Marian's going up to London, yes. She's going on Mrs Rushton's behalf, yes. But it's not, I assure you, to see a doctor or a shrink and certainly not to try to get her into an institution. She's not mentally ill. She may be disturbed, which of us isn't, but I assure you that she's quite sane enough to look after the shop this morning. The alternative is to close it, and as you know, trade is usually brisk on a Saturday morning. I'm quite willing to lock your door if you're afraid of her coming at you with an axe or something.'

'Don't treat me as though I'm senile. Would you pass me that library book, please? If I'm to be shut up here on my own all day, I'd better have another shot at it.'

'Mrs Rushton offered to come up to get you some lunch.'

'I'd rather you phoned Miss Morris.'

'That's exactly what I told her. "She's got a friend who'll come along," I said. I'll phone her now.'

He returned in less than a minute. 'She'll be here at half past twelve. She's going to pick up some fish and chips for you both on her way over.'

'I hope you told her plaice.'

'I did.'

'I certainly don't intend to eat cod. Or eel, rock-salmon or huss, or whatever they choose to call it.'

'Of course not. Right, well, I shall be off. I'll see you around five. Enjoy your book. And your plaice.'

'Miss Morris, you're an intelligent woman.'

'Moderately intelligent, I hope, Mrs Dainton.'

'Worked all your life amongst books?'

'That's right. Assistant librarian for nearly forty-five years.'

'Why is this area associated with magic? Can you tell me that?'

'Well now, many scholars believe that this town is situated on the site of ancient Arberth. And no place in Britain has stronger links with the supernatural. I suppose you've read the old legends, Mrs Dainton?'

'No, I can't say I have. Gerald Maitland lent me some boring old book a few years ago, but I failed to get into it.'

'Pity. It's old-fashioned, of course, but very moving in its own way. I learnt reams of it when I was at school. "And as they were sitting thus, lo, a peal of thunder, and with the magnitude of the peal, lo, a fall of mist coming, so that no one of them could see the other. And no manner of thing could they see: neither house nor beast nor smoke nor fire nor man nor dwelling, but the houses of the court empty, desolate, uninhabited, without man, without beast within them, their very companions lost." Sometimes I go out in the night and recite that, and when I get to the end of the passage I feel quite surprised that the town hasn't disappeared. That's how it takes me.'

'It may disappear next time,' Mrs Dainton said acidly. 'Take care.'

'But do you like all that stuff? Magic spells and so on?' she asked after a moment or two, fearing that she might have given offence.

'It's much more than that, though. It's about the wonder of love, about losing the one you love, about being brave, being resource- ful, being rewarded. And the people in it are very like the people you meet every day, brave or cowardly, boastful or modest, truthful or sly....But you know, Mr Maitland is the one who could answer your questions. He's become quite the authority on ancient Arberth.'

'Marian's friend was telling us that the people in those days worshipped Goddesses.'

'I've heard that. I don't suppose any one knows for certain. But I don't see why even our God shouldn't be female, do you?'

'God the Mother. What a laugh.'

'I'm inclined to agree with you, Mrs Dainton. Our Father. That springs more readily to the lips, somehow.'

'Otherwise, why should the scales be tipped against us as they are? Finished at fifty. Just when men are getting into their stride.'

'Yet we out-live men, on the whole.'

'That's our bad luck, as well.'

'Nonsense. I know I'm looking forward to a good long retirement. But there, I haven't had a husband to mourn after.'

'Neither have I.'

'Oh come now, Mrs Dainton. You're too fond of trying to shock. You don't fool me. You were a very loving wife, I'm sure.'

'I was a bitch of a wife.'

'You are a one, you are. Plenty of people pretend to be better than they are. You're one of the other sort. If you were the wicked woman you pretend to be, your son wouldn't be so careful of you, would he now? "Stay with her for an hour or two, Miss Morris, won't you, I don't want her to be lonely." He's so loving.'

'So loving he won't tell me where he's going today or what he's doing.'

'"Get her a nice piece of plaice, Miss Morris. She finds cod difficult to digest."'

'Why did you never get married, Miss Morris?'

'You've asked me that several times. My fiancé was killed during the war, Mrs Dainton. I never found anyone else, never really wanted anyone else. I suppose I got used to being on my own.'

'I never got used to it. I hated being on my own. Perhaps it was my lack of education. I never had any education, nothing that stuck anyway.'

'It's never too late, Mrs Dainton. Do you ever listen to Schools Radio? The programmes are very interesting. Schools Television is sometimes wonderful and Open University too. I couldn't quite follow the Theory of Relativity last year, but I'll give it another try in the autumn. We must keep the old brain cells active, you know, or they dry up. If you have a day without learning anything new, millions of them dry up and flake away like dandruff...Oh, now you're ready for your little nap. I'm talking too much as usual.'

'It's these damned tablets, that's what it is. I never used to sleep like a baby, every afternoon.'

'Sleep never harmed anyone, as far as I know.'

'Would you pass me my eiderdown?'

'Of course. What a pretty colour it is. So light, too.'

'Faded and old. Faded and old.'

'I'll slip out, Mrs Dainton.'

And Miss Morris tip-toed out into the tidy kitchen and began the washing-up.

Her face was soft and unlined, her eyes a clear blue, her hair sepia brown, like old photographs. Her seventeen-year-old navy-blue dress had once had a white collar, but she'd dispensed with it a few summers ago, finding it — to her surprise — frayed and rather yellow. She now put on some heavy china beads, cream, whenever she wore the dress, and always wondered, whenever she fastened the clasp, who had given them to her, and how long ago. Her brown sandals were the sort that children used to wear at that time when children wore the sensible low-heeled footwear their mothers chose for them.

Paul had left a five-pound note for her and a short message. 'Dear Miss Morris, Thank you so much, Paul.'

She counted out the right change for him and left it in a careful pile on the corner of the table.

He's a good son, she said to herself. And if he is one of these homosexuals, what does it matter?

It was Mrs Dainton who'd told her about it. She was always asking him whether he'd got a young lady and when he was thinking of getting married and so on, and one day, when he'd gone out, his mother had snapped at her. 'For God's sake, don't you know he's a queer?'

'I've always disliked that derogatory word, Mrs Dainton,' she'd said quietly. 'And I don't think it behoves you to use it. The only queer thing about Paul, it seems to me, is how loving and dutiful he is to such a difficult mother.'

She sighed. No, she hadn't actually said it. She seldom did say the sharp things that came into her mind, full of words like behoves and derogatory. Perhaps it would be better if she did.

She tutted to herself as she locked the door and left.

Mrs Dainton slept for an hour, sitting up in her chair, her faded eiderdown over her knees, the sun streaming in through the drawn curtains.

And when she woke, she immediately began to talk to herself again.

Take my Grandma, she said. What a wonderful woman she was. I do hope I take after you Grandma, I've always tried to. Not after Grandpa, so virtuous and careful of his pennies. Got up at half-past three on a Monday morning, Grandpa did, walked fourteen miles to get the train to take him to the mines, worked hard all week. Stayed in mean lodgings. Spent twopence a week on tobacco. Nothing on beer. Got back home three o'clock Saturday afternoon. Methodist church three times on Sunday. Up again half-past three the next Monday. What a way to live.

He didn't live long. He died before he was forty with nearly a hundred pound saved, a fortune in those days, for a miner, anyway. He must have half-starved his family and himself to have that much stashed away.

And what did my Grandma do then? Picture her, a small, middle-aged, dark-skinned woman, newly widowed. She went for a bloody holiday, that's what she did. The first she'd ever had. Took her four kids with her. Stayed away till every blessed penny was spent. Came back then, took in washing and kept hens and pretty near starved again, I suppose.

I used to go and stay with her when I was small. She smelled of chicken mess, but I was always fond of her because of that holiday my Dad had told me about.

'What did you do on your holiday, Gran?' I used to ask her. 'You and my Dad and my aunties?'

'We went for long walks along the cliffs. We paddled in the sea and every day we bought mackerel for our landlady to cook us for our tea. They were three a penny. Once we went out in a boat.

It was very near a hundred years ago. Queen Victoria's reign. Where's that commemoration mug? Can't see the date from here. Still in mourning she was, with her surly little face. When did her man die? Years and years before. True love. She screamed like a fishwife when he went, screamed and screamed. Perhaps it was rage. Perhaps no-one had ever defied her before.

When I was about, what, seventeen, my Grandma came to live with us. Came to die with us would be more the truth. How old would she have been? She seemed to me about a hundred. I remember one time she had a bit of an accident and she never wanted my mother to know. Even bold bad people like her were ashamed of their natural functions in those days. Wash my nightie for me will you, Alice? I'll give you sixpence when you gets me pension next week. I think I need a bit of a wipe down-under as well. I can manage if you brings me a drop of nice 'ot water an' a rag. Do you want me to help you? I asked. I'll pretend I'm a nurse. Come on, turn around. Her skin was like yellow chammy-leather, creased over her belly like another vest.

I don't remember the day she died. It's quite gone from me. I only remember the day I washed her bottom and her fanny and sprinkled Atter of Roses talcum over her and made her laugh.

She left me a white jug with a bunch of primroses on it. It means something to me, that jug. I like to think she got it on that holiday when she was in the money. Where is it? It's there, somewhere.

The war. Well I remember two world wars. I was only three months when the first one started but I remember two things about it. One was the vile taste of the stuff they called margarine, the other was.... damned if I remember the other. It may have been the street party we had when it was over. I was dressed up as Brittania. Almost all the girls were, but it was me got the prize, anyway. I was that sort, jumping up and down to be noticed, I suppose. I had my photograph in the paper.

The second war, 1939 to 1945. It was supposed to be hell on earth but for me it was a little bit of heaven.

Some nights when I can't sleep, I count all the lovely men-friends I had. I remember some little thing about all of them, the way they walked or talked, the way they smiled or smelled. Samuel Larch. An army private he was. I was in a pub with him having a drink in the bar and one of his mates leant across to flirt with me and he thumped him bang in the face. Knocked him over. He was sorry after, and bought him a drink. You've got a nasty temper, I said to him after it had all cooled down. I know I have, he said, and his face was the colour of dirty bath water. My old man killed my mother, he said after a bit. He swung for it and I'll finish up the same way. It was brave of him to tell me. He didn't think I'd go out with him after that, but I did. I never argued with him, though. Samuel is a strange name. Very Biblical.

I wonder when Paul will be coming back. I could really fancy a cup of tea.

EIGHT

Miss Morris had admired Gerald Maitland for fifteen years or more. When he gave lectures — with slides — in the Town Hall, she was always the first to buy a ticket and she had never missed any of his appearances on television. He'd always smiled at her in the library, but she'd never had the opportunity to speak to him, because the moment he appeared through the door, the chief librarian would hurry over to attend to him. 'Allow me, Miss Morris,' Mr Cynfab-Jones would say in his low, measured tones, 'I'll see to Mr Maitland.'

Whenever they met in the street, though, she would be sure to catch his eye so that he would have to raise his hat to her as he passed. She never dreamed that their relationship would get beyond that stage.

Yet, when she let herself out of the antique shop shortly after half-past one on that Saturday afternoon and noticed him looking in at the window, she approached him as though they were old friends. 'Mr Maitland,' she said. 'Well now, what a coincidence. I've just been talking about you.'

'Indeed,' Mr Maitland said, quite unperturbed it seemed, at being approached with such familiarity. 'You must tell me more Miss Morris.' (She gave a little gasp, which she quickly turned into a cough, when she realised he knew her name.) 'Are you walking up the hill? Good. The shop closes for the afternoon, I suppose?'

'Yes, it closes at one on a Saturday. It's a good antique shop isn't it? We're fortunate to have it in a town of this size. It brings us a lot of trade, I suppose. They tell me that people come here from as far as Swansea and Carmarthen.'

'Yes. Dainton is beginning to show some interest in local antiquarian books, that's what people come for, no doubt. You have to specialise these days if you want to get anywhere.'

They walked up the road together, Miss Morris still not quite able to credit her own daring.

'You must be a great help to him in that line,' she ventured to suppose, with rather a coy smile.

'I've...Well, I've done... er... a little, perhaps.' (It had never occurred to him to do anything but buy the odd book or two.)

How modest he was, Miss Morris thought. It only went to show. Great men were always humble.

Not being much given to flattery, she stumbled over the next sentence. 'Mrs Dainton and I were discussing your...knowledge... and scholarship, Mr Maitland. Mr Dainton had to be out today and I've just been giving her a spot of lunch.'

'Mrs Dainton! Mrs Dainton's not very interested in much apart from gossip, I'm afraid.'

'Oh no, you're wrong. It's rubbing off on her. It does, doesn't it? Scholarship, I mean. It's a light casting a glow on all around. It would be surprising, I think, if our whole town was not enlightened to some extent.'

Gerald Maitland cast a quick glance in her direction. She seemed serious and quite sober.

'Thank you.' he said, pulling at his tie. (It was abysmally hot.) 'I'm gratified that you have such regard for... for... what small contribution...er...I've been able to make... er... to the cultural life of the town.'

'Oh Mr Maitland. A small contribution! Whenever you treat us to one of your talks we hang on your every word.' Gerald Maitland recalled, without rancour, that thirteen people had been present at his last lecture, one being his daily help and one the caretaker of the hall. Marian had described the talk as 'awfully well-judged, not too obscure, not too patronising.' It was gratifying to think that one among the thirteen had 'hung on his every word.'

'You see, I love the old legends,' Eira Morris said, and her voice was that of a lover or a young mother speaking of her new-born.

Gerald Maitland stopped dead. Who could have dreamt that this rather plain — he shot her another glance, was she rather plain? Not exactly, well...who could have dreamt that this certainly elderly if rather charming woman in shapeless dress and fawn cardigan, could sound so passionate?

'I have a copy of the Cockerel Press edition,' he said in a slightly hesitant voice.

'Oh,' she said. The little round sound floated between them for a moment.

He drew a deep breath. 'Would you care to see it? Perhaps you'd like to come in for a drink?'

'Well indeed, I'd love a cup of tea.'

They walked the rest of the way in silence, Gerald Maitland surprised and Eira Morris almost overwhelmed by the turn of events.

'Pre-Christian. Oh yes, without a doubt. What Christianity did was to over-turn the old themes by its emphasis on chastity. For instance, in the earliest oral versions, the king of the Underworld would have begotten the wonder-child on the earthly woman. It would have been quite straightforward. But imagine the effect of the early church on this story....'

It was wonderful, Miss Morris thought, the way he was talking to her. As though, well, as though she mattered. Almost as though he wanted to impress her; she who was already his ardent admirer.

She kept her eyes on him as he talked. She couldn't help thinking that he seemed to have aged in the last year, his greying hair had become silvery, his eyes drooped. Hadn't he become too thin? And instead of being full of his usual self-assurance, he seemed worried, almost burdened. Perhaps it was only the heat of the afternoon. Even outside it was so close that the scent of the orange blossom was as heavy as in an airless room.

His discourse came to an end. Unwilling to move while he was talking, she now reached again for her cup of tea.

'Will you do something for me, Miss Morris?'

'If I can.' Her heart fluttered.

'Will you read a few passages for me in Welsh? I've taught myself a little over the years, but I'm still not fluent. This is one of my favourite parts.'

They were sitting on a garden seat flanked by small round bay trees in cast-iron containers. He was wearing a white panama hat and had insisted on finding an old straw hat for her, though they were in the shade of the large fig tree which grew against the wall.

The garden was lovely. She'd never seen anything remotely like it. Wherever she looked, in whatever direction, she encountered a careful arrangement of grey stone and green leaf, with here and there a flaunt of pink or yellow. The slim thrushes spearing the few square yards of barbered grass seemed as decorative as peacocks. Even the spilled white petals on the terrace and the lichen, in gold spots like coins, seemed part of the overall design.

The passage he asked her to read was how Lleu's wife — fashioned from flowers by Gwydion the magician — fell in love with the huntsman, Gronw Pebyr, and plotted her husband's death, and how

Gwydion for punishment, turned her into an owl.

She read steadily for several minutes.

She had a low clear voice.

'I'm glad you like that story,' she said after she had finished. 'You see, it was the first I ever heard. It was in my elementary school, when I was six or seven. Oh, I've liked owls ever since. They do have flower faces, don't they? And at night they cry Gronw, Gronw, for their lost love.'

'Gronoooo, Gronoooo,' Gerald Maitland echoed. 'Yes. Charming.'

'I hope there's no-one listening to us,' Eira Morris whispered.

'Gronoo-oo. Gronoo-oo.' Gerald Maitland hooted over the town.

They grew silent.

Where had Sally Rushton disappeared to, Gerald wondered. Marian had told him about her trip to London and of how Sally was going to to take over the shop in her absence, and he had sat on the seat outside the library for over half an hour — from five to one until half-past — hoping to catch her leaving. At last he'd wandered over to see if she'd forgotten the time, and had found the shop already closed.

And the disappointment of missing her had been acute. No fool like an old fool, he told himself, staring at the clocks and barometers in the window. (Too late, the clocks, all said, while the barometers foretold the end of all weather.)

He'd hoped to take her to Tenby for lunch and afterwards to see the Celtic Cross in the nearby churchyard of Penally.

Idiot, he told himself. What had he hoped for? For nothing. Nothing. He didn't even like the woman. It was habit, that was all, the undeviating habit of a lifetime. Old as he was, he still seemed to crave the proximity of a beautiful woman.

But he must rouse himself, he thought, to get a spot of lunch. This wouldn't do at all, he thought, as his eyelids dropped.

When he was asleep, and she loath to disturb him, Miss Morris sat with her hands in her lap and remembered her sweetheart, Glyn Parry from Llanddu, who'd been killed in Burma nearly fifty years before. She seldom thought of him now; his memory, a half-forgotten tune, only occasionally disturbing the surface of her mind.

Her parents hadn't approved of him. She was too good, they said to marry into the haulier business; she with the County School behind her and all the money they'd spent on her piano lessons.

But she would have married him, all the same. If he'd come back.

He was tall, round-shouldered because of his height and his job, with a large, shaggy head and sad blue eyes. He was too shy to arrange meetings, he'd just turn up from time to time; outside the library at five o' clock on a Saturday afternoon or occasionally after chapel on a fine summer evening.

She remembered with shame how she'd once berated him because he never let her know when she could expect him, and how he'd blushed and mumbled about the nine miles he had to cycle — no distance he'd said, except after heavy rain when the mile-long farm track from their house was muddy and almost impassable. You musn't come so often, she'd said, then, and he'd smiled the nice slow smile that changed his face.

They'd walked on the hills in the summer, gone to the cinema, whatever the film, in the winter and rough weather.

What had they talked about? Nothing much that she could remember; her job in the library, her parents, his parents and brothers and sisters — none of whom she'd ever met — places he'd gone to that week in the lorry. They liked the same programmes on the wireless. When she listened to the poetry contest on a Tuesday evening or to the play on a Wednesday, she liked to think that he would be listening too, and that they would discuss them — or at least she would, he never said much — when they'd next meet. They never talked about love,

The love in their affair had only begun after he'd been called up and sent to England to begin his training. Then his letters had been full of his longing for her. Things he had never dared to speak, he wrote with an ease and fluency that surprised her. He agonised about all the kisses he had never given her for fear she would repulse him. 'I didn't dare hope,' he wrote, 'that my feelings for you would be returned.'

'They are returned,' she confessed in her reply, trembling at the strength of them. 'I love you and I'll wait for you.'

A few months and many letters later, he'd sent her an engage-ment ring, a narrow gold band with three tiny diamonds and she'd worn it in spite of her mother's disapproval. 'Your father gave me a solitaire,' her mother'd said with a sniff. 'Why couldn't you get yourself a bank-clerk or a teacher? Throwing yourself away, that's what you're doing, you with your French and your German, never mind your piano.'

All the same, he'd been invited to the house when he came home for his first leave.

Her mother had made an elaborate meal, with knives and forks laid out in pairs like in a hotel; she was sure it was only to embarrass him. It had been an awkward evening, but they'd survived it, and afterwards she'd taken him out as far as the gate and he'd kissed her, though not as ardently as he did in his letters.

And within another six months he was sent to India and before the end of the year he was dead.

And she'd gathered together all his precious letters and momentos and had burned them in the garden. It had been like a memorial service for him, with her the only mourner.

And every year after that she'd become a little more solid in appearance, a little more like her mother and her grandmother. She'd let herself go, she supposed. She sighed. She'd had a perm, once, but felt as though she'd got a bird's nest stuck on her head. Face cream made her feel sticky. Anyway, she'd got her health and strength she told herself, and those were the important things.

I wonder if I'd have made him a good wife, she thought, sitting under the fig tree in the sun. Would I have become impatient with his slow ways and his dull job? Would I have made him unhappy?

Gerald Maitland woke with a start.

'I must go,' she said, feeling angry with herself because she'd fawned over him earlier.

He led her through the cool house to the front door.

'I do hope you'll call again,' he said. 'I'm trying to write a book and your enthusiasm could help me enormously. Shall I give you a ring to suggest a time?'

The first rumble of distant thunder could be heard as she reached her own small house.

NINE

On the train to London, Marian felt sick with apprehension. How had Sally managed to persuade her into going on this fool's errand?

She had sobbed and begged, that was how, used all her considerable wiles. 'I've got no-one else I can ask. Please Marian, do this one thing for me and I'll never, never ask you to do anything else. You've always been my best friend, Marian. It won't be too difficult for you, surely. You've only got to tell him how I feel about him, that I want him back. He doesn't realise how I feel about him. '

'But you told me you'd begged him to stay.'

'He thought I was trying to upset his plans, I think, after he'd finally decided. It might have been that. He took no notice, anyway. And you see, I've never been able to write in case he showed *her* the letter. You're my only hope, Marian. I want him to come back to me. This girl he's living with is.. .well, a negligible person. Virginia's met her several times. She says she's ordinary.'

But men often liked ordinary women best, Marian had thought, though she hadn't had the heart to say so. Perhaps Alan had had altogether too much of brilliance and beauty.

She'd made one excuse after another. 'But how will I contact him? What if 'she' answers the phone? Where could he meet me without arousing 'her' suspicion?'

It would be straightforward, perfectly easy and straightforward. 'She' was away for a fortnight, taking a school orchestra on a tour of Germany. Alan had written to Virginia telling her how lonely he'd be, suggesting that she visited him while he was on his own. Virginia had wondered whether the letter could possibly be a ploy to get Sally to contact him, but Sally was too nervous to take that step. She needed an intermediary. And she'd immediately thought of Marian, her oldest and dearest friend, as the best and indeed the only possible go-between.

'Sally asked me to call on you. She's staying with me at the moment. At my cottage in Pembrokeshire.' Marian rehearsed her opening words. Should she say that Sally was ill? Perhaps it wasn't strictly true, but she certainly seemed to be seriously disturbed.

'Say I want him to come back to me.' Somehow Sally seemed to think these words would have an immediate and dramatic effect on Alan. Marian feared she might even be counting on his accompanying her back on the evening train .

She's a great responsibility, Marian kept telling herself. Now that Johnny and Tim are off my hands to some extent, this is what happens. Anyway, I never had to sort out their personal problems. Beyond telling the odd girlfriend they weren't in when they were, and on one occasion keeping one talking at the front door while another was being dispatched from the back. I've had absolutely no experience.

Also, I always found Alan difficult to talk to, I've never really hit it off with small, shy men. Being shy myself, I've always got on much better with the extrovert types who make silly jokes to put you at your ease and say the first banal thing that comes into their heads; the ones Sally says are ineffectual and of no account.

I couldn't sleep last night for worrying and I'm hopeless after a wakeful night. Oh, how I wish I was on the journey back. No good can come of this.

When she arrived, she had lunch at the Paddington Hotel. Smoked salmon paté, lamb, new potatoes and fresh peas, blackcurrant cheesecake and cream, a good eight hundred calories she didn't need, just to stop her feeling so nervous.

'Marian! How super to see you. Do come in. Excuse the mess. I'm trying to get the sitting-room decorated.'

Alan had changed. He seemed to have grown taller if that was possible. He kissed her warmly and fussed over her. He was certainly no longer shy.

'Why don't we go out into the garden? What there is of it. It's not much bigger than a bath towel, but at least it gets the sun in the afternoon. I'll bring out some cushions, the chairs aren't too comfortable. Will you excuse me while I wash my hands and get out of this overall? It *is* good to see you.' He kissed her again.

Of course it was partly his hair. In the past it had always been uncompromisingly short. She seemed to remember Sally saying that he had it cut regularly every fortnight at the same barber in the city. Now, while not exactly long, it was...well...floppy. It made him look, not handsome, perhaps, but certainly boyish and attractive.

When he came back to the garden, he was wearing tight jeans and a bright yellow T-shirt. It was another shock.

'You'll have a cup of tea, Marian?' (She was surprised not to be offered coke.) 'I was just thinking of making one. Oh, it is good to see you. Milk or lemon?'

And then he was gone again, without letting her get a word in.

Anyway, why shouldn't he have changed his image? He was probably finding his own personality at last. Previously he'd been not much more than Sally's fashion accessory; the slim,dark, formally-dressed man successful women always had hovering in the background. Why on earth shouldn't he be wearing a silver chain round his neck? Why shouldn't he be wearing Reebok trainers?

Oh God, he'd switched on a radio in the kitchen. Loud teenage music — the sort which always drove her to curse and bang on walls — was blaring out over the garden. It seemed the last straw. Sally asked me to call on you, she said to herself miserably, sweating and longing to get away.

He came back, bringing the transistor with him on the tray. 'You don't like the Pixies?' he asked her.

'No.'

He turned it off. Silence. 'I'm not mad on them, either. I suppose I was trying to impress you.'

'Why?'

He smiled, but didn't answer.

She took a sip of the delicately-flavoured tea, then a deep breath. 'I've come about Sally,' she said.

'Oh.' His face fell. 'I see. About Sally.'

'She's very upset...you know...very distressed.'

He leaned back in the plastic picnic chair, closing his eyes against the sun. It was as if he hadn't heard her.

She wondered whether to repeat herself. Was now perhaps the time to trot out the phrase 'mentally disturbed'?

Why didn't he say something? Make some sort of response? Was he ill? The heat was certainly oppressive.

'I thought you'd just decided to look me up,' he said at last. 'I thought perhaps Virginia had been in touch with you. I've so missed seeing you, Marian. I've always thought of you as a very special friend.'

'I've missed seeing you, too,' she said. (She hadn't, of course. She'd only ever thought of him as Sally's husband, never as a friend in his own right.)

'I don't know anyone in this crappy neighbourhood. I haven't spoken to anyone all week, except at work. But this morning, I had a premonition that something good was going to happen, and when I saw you on the doorstep I felt so happy. Will you have another cup of tea?'

'Please.'

The afternoon, Marian told herself, was going from bad to worse.

She stirred her tea vigorously. She simply had to get back to the purpose of her visit.

'Sally's staying with me at the moment,' she said. 'In my cottage in Pembrokeshire.'

He looked away again.

'Why don't you come down for a few days?' she found herself saying. 'It would be so nice.'

He sat up. 'I'd love to. I'd really love to,'

Marian felt elated. It wasn't what she'd planned, but it seemed a good idea.

'When could you come?'

'Well obviously not while Sally's there. I could come at any other time.'

She had to explain herself, awkward though it was. 'But Alan, that was the idea. To bring you two together. You should never have parted. She's missing you desperately. She wants you to come back to her.'

There was another long silence.

'I couldn't,' Alan said at last. 'How could you ask me to? She's a sick woman.'

'But only because you left her. She needs you. She loves you.'

'Is that what she told you?'

'Yes. She's had at least one crying bout every day since she's been with me.'

'But it's not for me, Marian, I promise you. She's done quite a lot of crying for one reason or another, I know. And, yes, she'd like me back, but only because she can't find anyone else to put up with her, I know that, too. And I can't take any more, or I'll end up as mad as she is.'

82

'Do you really think she's mentally ill?'

'Of course she is. She's been mentally ill for at least four years. Ever since...well...ever since...'

'Ever since what, Alan?'

'Ever since she had that abortion...Marian, hasn't she even told you about the abortion she had? Hasn't she told you anything? I always thought you knew *something* about it all?'

Marian wiped her forehead. The weather was so close and sticky; she felt the past pressing in on her. There were so many things she didn't understand, so many things she hadn't been told, hadn't bothered to think about. Why hadn't Sally told her that she'd gone through an abortion? Why hadn't Alan let her know, so that she'd have been able to be at hand to support her? Why ever was Alan looking at her so strangely? Why ever...? Her throat tightened.

'It was Dickie's baby, wasn't it?' Marian asked.

She felt as though she'd known about it all along, carried the weight of it about her with her for years. 'Aren't I a fool? It's all settled into place now. They had an affair for years, didn't they? I think I half knew about it all along.'

Alan took her hand and pressed it. 'I thought she'd have at least told you about the abortion,' he said.

'They should have told me about it,' she said. 'How dared they have kept it from me? I wouldn't have let her have it. Why did she? Whose decision was it?'

Alan flinched at her anger. 'Certainly not mine,' he said.' And I can't say I much want to discuss it all again. She had the abortion and regretted it afterwards. That's all there was to it.'

He looked suddenly tired: she could see how he would look when he was old. She tried to smile at him to show she was on his side, that she didn't blame him for anything...Except that he should have let her know.

'What could you have done?' Alan asked, as though reading her mind. 'What solution was there? Would you have given Dickie up? Begged him to marry Sally? That's what she wanted. That's the only thing that would have satisfied her.'

Marian couldn't answer.'How long did you know about their affair?' she asked.

'Oh, for years. Of course they kept promising to break it off and I always believed them. To be honest, I think Dickie did try to break with her. He used to escape to the cottage saying it was over, but when he came back it always started again.'

'That holiday in the South of France? Was that when it started? That day they were so late getting back from their shopping trip?'

'Round about that time, I think. How long ago was that?'

'John would have been about seven. Yes, I can remember the snaps I took, his two front teeth were missing, he'd have been about seven. Fourteen years ago.'

Alan put his arm around her.

'He loved you,' he said. 'And the boys. It was a classic case of a man torn in two. Oh God, why did I have to do this to you?'

Marian couldn't stop crying, now that she'd started. Those vividly recalled holiday snapshots made it all so poignant. They'd all looked so happy. And the children so beautiful; Johnny, all his ribs showing and his toothless grin, Virginia, fair as a mermaid, her long hair half way down her back, and little Tim, baby-cheeked and solemn. And she so innocent.

Alan put both his arms round her and let her cry.

'I was so trusting,' she said. 'Such a fool.'

'Trusting and trustworthy. The two things go together.'

'A fool. If I hadn't been so complacent — or so afraid of finding out the truth, I'm not sure which it was — things would have come to a head, everything would have been resolved, one way or another.'

'You musn't think that. I thought that, when I first found out about them. But nothing was ever resolved. They decided this, they promised that, but everything started again and went on as before. Don't blame yourself. What good does it do? You were trusting and innocent. Thank God for people like you.'

Marian drew away from him and blew her nose.

'Alan, you should have told me about it. Why should you have had to go through everything on your own?'

'I don't even know why I went through it. I know I threatened to end the marriange often enough when I found out they were still seeing each other, but she could always get round me: she needed me. She loved me. Her passion for Dickie didn't alter the way she felt for me. We had to think of Virginia. We were a family. It was years before I finally realised that she would have been ready enough to let me go if she could have been sure of Dickie. It was the shame and humiliation of being left with no-one that she couldn't take. And she's the same now. She's a very complex character, Marian; dangerous, as all people are who can't put anything above their own desires.'

They fell silent again, thinking their own thoughts.

Marian thought about Dickie. She couldn't feel much anger or bitterness towards him; she supposed it was because he was so safely dead. However much he'd cheated and lied, put their marriage at risk, he'd finished up with nothing. Pity was all she could feel for him, and the poor, sad remnants of love. Tears scalded her eyes as she thought of him; out of reach of either her love or forgiveness.

Alan was thinking of Marian. He was beyond feeling anything for Sally. He had loved her extravagantly — in the way she demanded to be loved — but by this time every drop of feeling had been squeezed out of him. He felt distressed that he had even to think and talk of her again. Only for Marian's sake would he do so.

'I thought Dickie's death could bring us together,' he said. 'For the first time I realised how much she'd loved him — previously I'd always considered her feelings for him a sort of greed — and because I realised she was capable of love, I felt sympathy with her again; fell in love with her again, I suppose. For a time she really did seem 'ennobled' by suffering. But of course it didn't last. Soon — within about six months, I think — she started having other affairs, behaving with a sort of reckless desperation which was very hard to put up with. We went on holiday to Portugal at about this time. Poor Virginia was with us.'

For a time he sat back in his chair, unable to continue.

'Don't distress yourself,' Marian said. 'I can imagine the sort of thing that happened.'

'She didn't care, simply didn't care enough, by that time, to try to conceal it even from the chap's wife, who was about six or seven months pregnant. It was a ghastly holiday. Virginia and I seemed to be left with the wife — a nice little thing in her early twenties with one of those plump little-girl faces that pregnant women often have — all pretending like mad we didn't know what was going on. Virginia always refused to come on holiday with us after that and I can't say I blamed her.'

'I was always very fond of Virginia,' Marian said, pleased to be able to change the subject. 'We phoned her last night. She said she'd try to come down next weekend. I do hope she manages it. I'm so looking forward to seeing her again.'

'Has Sally mentioned her boy-friend? He came to stay with us for a few days last year. The first time we'd met him. Jess. Six or seven years older than her. An artist of some sort.' Alan threw his eyes to the sky. 'The sort of rough fellow you hope will be better than he looks because he can't be worse. Sally kept moaning about how vulgar he was, his nails were filthy and he sucked his tea and he kept saying Rubbish to everything she said...And then what do you think happened?'

'She fell for him,' Marian said promptly.

'I don't know about that, but she certainly made one hell of a pass at him.'

'And what happened?'

'Nothing. Absolutely nothing. It was a moment of truth for her, I think. This very animal sort of man actually laughed off her advances, showed quite clearly that he preferred Virginia — who's not at all pretty or attractive in any conventional way. The odd thing was that Virginia seemed able to ignore the whole thing. I think she'd have been able to shrug it off even if he *had* slept with Sally.'

Marian sighed. 'Love isn't as important to these youngsters as it was to us — to our generation, I mean. Well, it doesn't have to be, does it? They're not even pretending that it's something for a lifetime.'

'It was Sally who wasn't able to get over it,' Alan said. 'It was Sally who was devastated.'

Was there a hint of satisfaction in his voice? 'Were you pleased?' Marian asked him.

'No,' he said firmly. And then, 'Yes, of course I was fucking pleased. I'm not a saint.'

The storm broke over them with ferocious suddenness, the rain drenching them before they'd managed to make the ten or twelve yards to the house.

They closed the door against the deluge and then stood at the kitchen window watching the lightning whipping across the sky.

'You're soaked,' Alan said. 'I'll fetch you a towel. 'You should get changed.'

'I'm all right. Honestly.'

When he brought the towel she only laid it round her shoulders and went on watching the sky.

The first thunder-clap seemed immediately above their heads.

They drew together and when they clasped each other's hands it seemed the most natural thing in the world.

They stood by the window until the worst of the storm was over.

TEN

Paul Dainton's first call on that Saturday morning was at the Mill House in Bryn Tirion, a village three miles away. Long unoccupied and fallen into that state of disrepair which estate agents categorise as 'needing sympathetic restoration', it had recently come on the market, and he was determined to buy it.

It was in a superb position for an antique business, rural, densely green, yet only two or three hundred yards off the main coast road. There was ample living accommodation — he'd already been shown round it — as well as a large double-room which would make an excellent showroom.

As he approached it again, his spirits soared. The early morning haze had lifted and the sky was a tender, cloudless, summer blue.

He got out of the car. The house's uncompromising squareness and solidity seemed to him beautiful. Everything about it whispered, or rather shouted, class. This is it, he said to himself, this is most definitely it.

The drifts of willow herb in what had once been a small front garden, brought out pink and mauve shades in the sombre grey stone of the house. Honeysuckle fell from an archway leading to the door. I'll leave all this exactly as it is, he told himself, nothing could improve on this ragged wilderness, the overgrown shrub roses, the mint and thyme in the long grass, lost except for their sharp green scents, bindweed like carnival garlands in the hedges. Mill House Antiques, he said to himself, sounding like someone reciting a poem in a dream.

After spending ten minutes or so walking round the house and the outbuildings, peering through windows at brown rooms with uneven oak floors and wide doorways, he sauntered down to the river. An eighteenth century house set in a grassy garden at the river's edge, he said to himself. (Leafy garden? Verdant garden?) Oh, and Member of the Antiques Guild, as well.

The river was green and full. Swallows dived onto the surface, slicing the air within a few feet of him. The branches of the willows were reflected, gently rippling, in the water. Every blade of grass quivered with colour. This is it, he said again, standing on the bank as though he wanted to take root there.

He'd never felt closer to happiness. He was going to work hard and make a success of his life. He now had the incentive he'd always searched for.

He'd had many love-affairs, some, he admitted, more heady and passionate than his present one, but he'd recently felt a deep desire to settle down, and in Gareth he knew he'd found someone he could trust.

Gareth, several years younger than he was, was attractive without having the flaunting physical presence which caused heads to turn. In any case, he wasn't a flirt, but a steady, sensible country boy who'd never tangled in the underground scene as he himself had earlier on. Paul didn't often care to admit even to himself, that the reason he and his mother had moved to such a remote spot in South-West Wales was that he'd once got into trouble with the police. Four months was what he'd actually served. How little it sounded and how frightfully endless it had seemed, with all the humiliation of being treated as a pervert, instead of a person looking for another person, not to cheat or injure, but only to love.

It was Gareth's decision, a few weeks earlier, to leave his wife and two children and throw in his lot with him, that had brought about this decision to move up in the world. There was no way he was going to let Gareth join him in the poky little flat over the High Street shop.

Happy though he was, he realised that he had three outstanding problems.

The first was financial and didn't worry him over-much on that lovely morning. There were invariably ways and means, he told himself. His bank manager had agreed that the asking-price for Mill House was reasonable, though at least twice what he was likely to get for his shop, which was — another problem — in his mother's name. Still, since she was always urging him to think big, she was hardly likely to refuse him such a wonderful opportunity for expansion. Would he have to take out a mortgage to cover the remainder of the purchase money plus that needed for essential repairs? Or should he offer Marian a partnership? Or even Gerald Maitland? It required careful thought.

He knew that he himself would have to work far harder. He'd have to attend all the Sales that Marian marked for him every week. He'd have to buy and borrow books and magazines and make a determined effort to study them. He'd have to visit stately homes and museums. His flair could only get him so far; with much higher overheads and probably a large mortgage, his grip on the subject would have to be sure. A great deal of hard graft, he told himself.

As though to husband his energy, he sat down on the bank, his back against a tree.

The second problem was Gareth's wife, Susan. On the Wednesday of the present week, Gareth had managed to tell her about Paul; had broken the news that he intended to leave her in order to live with him.

Paul had never met Susan and had rarely thought about her. He'd accepted Gareth's assurances that the marriage had been ill-conceived and was virtually over.

However, Susan had obviously not shared Gareth's view. She had cried for a day and a night and had refused to accept that he was leaving her. 'You've got to come here on Saturday,' Gareth had written in his last letter. 'She insists on talking to you. You must come, Paul, or I'll never be able to go through with it.'

The thought of seeing Susan, though not an event to anticipate with any pleasure, caused Paul no more than mild irritation. Nobody can want to continue a relationship which is dead, he told himself. And now that he'd derived courage and determination from seeing Mill House again, he was ready to meet her. He took a few deep breaths, a last look at the river, and walked towards his car. He'd promised to be with Gareth by eleven.

The third problem, the one which loomed largest, was his mother.

I'm too soft-hearted, that's my trouble, he told himself as he started the car. I'd be a rich man now if it wasn't for this sentimental streak in my nature. I can't even cheat people. Well, not enough. I just can't look someone in the eye and say I'll give you a fiver for it, if I know perfectly well it's worth a whole lot more. Especially with old people, and after all, they've got the best antiques haven't they, stands to reason. When they come in with their terrible shiny clothes and their runny eyes, I'll give them almost as much as the bleedin' thing's worth. Yes, I get some bargains in Auction Sales from time to time, but when I buy cheap, half the time I'll sell without making a decent profit. A soft heart is an awful liability.

Well, that's how I've got landed with her. She can't do a thing for herself and she's awkward as they come. She'll make Gareth's life a misery, getting him to listen to all her old stories — lies, half of them — and making him feel guilty whenever he goes out. She'd be much better off with any of her other children, but she can't get on with them, and instead of standing firm and saying, You've got to bloody learn to get on with them, people of your age shouldn't be so bloody choosey, I just buckle under and say, OK, don't bother with them. Your home is with me. I need my head examined, I really do.

It isn't as if I ever really loved her, not that much anyway. Lots of boys worship their mothers. Not me. You could never depend on her. Sometimes she'd be in a great mood. I could stay home from school, have my breakfast in bed, she'd buy me comics and Smarties and make me Sunmaid raisin sandwiches for my tea. Other times, I'd be sent off to school with a streaming cold and she wouldn't even be there when I got back, only Eleanor, who'd be about seventeen I suppose, too old to argue with anyway, waiting for me with fish pie or some other poisonous dish she'd learnt to make at school, and insisting I went to bed at half-past seven. They were all too old to be of any use. Laura and Richard were even worse than Eleanor. Other kids had brothers and sisters who'd play with them. Mine were like a step-family, always moaning about me. You never let us leave our dinner, you never took us to the pictures, you never let us come to bed with you.

Yes she sometimes took me to the cinema with her, but it wasn't all that great. It always had to be films she wanted to see. Lust in the Dust. That sort. I got never to see things the other kids talked about, science fiction and moon monsters. My teacher, Miss Harrison, used to be really shocked when I told her about some of the things I'd seen. She even wrote to my mother about one of them. I think it was Diana Dors in a condemned cell because she'd killed her husband. Of course she wrote back and told her where to get off. A fine film she said, which might teach him a thing or two. Naturally, she was always ready to give Miss Harrison and any other of my teachers the benefit of her advice. God, it used to embarrass me.

Yes, she used to let me sleep with her sometimes, too, when it suited her. Usually when it was very cold. Probably saved her the trouble of getting a hot-water bottle. It was quite nice anyway, I'll admit that. Her bed was very soft and smelt of face cream and talcum powder and humbugs. Why can you eat sweets in bed and, not me, I'd ask her. Because, she'd say. No excuse or explanation. That was typical of her, that was.

Then came the time she said I was too old to sleep with her any longer. I didn't care too much. I'd often find myself with only a few inches of bed and no blankets. Mother-love they call it.

But one night after I'd had this horrible nightmare about being chased down a lift shaft by some of the boys from the Big School, I crept to her room and pushed in beside her, hoping she wouldn't wake up and send me away. No, she says. No Paul, go back to your own bed at once. No Paul.

Well, I was too frightened to obey her. I just pushed my way in, but then it was almost worse than the nightmare, because there, half way down her bed, was my father, naked and furious. Of course I started bawling...and was glad to rush back to my own bed to cool off. And after a while I thought it must have been another nightmare, because my mother and father were divorced and he'd got married again to this silly fat woman we had to call Aunt Elspeth, and my mother hated him and wouldn't even talk to him when he came over to fetch us to have Sunday dinner with them in their ugly red-brick house in the posh part of town.

'Hey, was that my Dad in bed with you the other night?' I asked her a few nights later, when she'd been to the pictures and to the pub on the way home, and was consequently in a playful, affectionate mood.

'And what if it was,' she said, ruffling my hair in a way she knew I detested. 'He's still my lawful wedded husband in the eyes of God.'

'It was horrible. He had his arms round your legs. You could have smothered him.'

She laughed at me, a long tinkly laugh, so that I felt hot and ashamed and affronted. Sometimes I hated her. I still do from time to time.

She was never easy. Living with her was like living with the weather. And now she's got even worse. She's eighty something and her arthritis gets her down and she mopes and wheedles and soon she won't even be able to take herself to the loo.

There's an Old People's Home in Garthowen, a Rest Home they call it. I went to look it over the other week. The matron was very understanding. She may not like the thought of coming here, she said, but once she's here, she'll be as happy as a sandboy. Oh Christ, it was just what they used to tell my mother when she used to try to leave me in the Infants class — and I was never happy as a bleedin' sandboy. Anyway, she took me over the whole place, showed me the dining room and the sitting room and even the bedrooms and bathrooms. It was all very clean and pleasant. Like a hotel really. Well, a third-grade hotel. I can't say the residents looked all that happy, but what have old people got to be happy about, when you come to think of it. Of course I told the matron I'd be getting in touch with her, but I never did.

It was the thought of telling the old girl, I suppose. I couldn't do it. How do you start? How do you bring up a subject like that? It's beyond me, I can tell you.

And yet I can't let her spoil everything between me and Gareth. She could do it without even trying. Oh, I suppose she'll have to come with us. And I suppose she'll have to stay with us, too, until one of us drops dead.

And I bet it won't be her, Paul was saying to himself as he turned into the council estate in Tenby where Gareth lived.

Though it was a small estate, it took him a long time to find Gareth's house. Perhaps he wasn't over-anxious to reach it.

He parked the car and walked up the path. The front garden was small and pretty, with clumps of old fashioned flowers; marigolds, sweet-williams, snapdragons and batchelors buttons. He realised that he was seeing everything with extraordinary clarity and hoped it wasn't going to be the beginning of one of his headaches.

The front door was closed, and had an unused look. It seemed to Paul like a symbol, like some locked door in a dream. For the first time he wondered whether he should have come.

He rang the bell and the door was immediately opened by Gareth, who must have been waiting for him. He was looking strained and pale. Why doesn't he get out into the sun, Paul wondered as he looked at him. He needs a holiday. We both do.

'Come in,' Gareth said, 'We've been waiting for you.' He didn't smile or even look at him.

The front room had a faint smell of damp and furniture polish. It was an ugly room, Paul thought, with some satisfaction. A red carpet with a swirling design of greys and yellows, a brown three-piece suite in some shiny vinyl material, a nasty little grate. 'The children are with her mother,' Gareth said. 'We thought it would be better. Sit down for God's sake.'

Paul sat on a hard brown armchair and smiled at him. 'Cheer up,'

93

he said, 'It's not the end of the world.'

'Susan's getting us some coffee,' Gareth said, looking as though it was.

Paul saw the photograph, then. Two smiling boys with a look of Gareth.

'Tom and Gwyn,' Gareth said, following his eyes. 'Taken last Christmas.'

Another silence.

When Susan came in with the coffee it was almost a relief.

She was much younger than Paul had expected, younger and prettier. (He'd pictured her as a faded woman in an overall.) She seemed enviably composed.

'I'm Paul Dainton,' Paul said, since Gareth didn't seem inclined to say anything. 'This is a very painful meeting. I'm not enjoying it, I assure you.'

'I can't stop Gareth leaving me,' Susan said, with no preliminaries, 'But I want you to see what you're breaking up. I want you to see me and the boys, so that you'll think of us from time to time. That's only fair.'

'The boys are with your mother,' Gareth said.

'She's bringing them back in half an hour. When we've had our talk. Do you take sugar?'

Paul said he did. He couldn't think of anything else to say.

Neither could Gareth.

But Susan suffered no such disability. 'I want you to see our wedding photograph,' she said, as soon as she'd passed them their cups of coffee. 'If I put it here on the table you can have a good look at it, can't you. Seven years ago we got married. It wasn't a rushed affair either. We'd been engaged a year, courting a year and half. I was just seventeen when I met Gareth. He was eighteen. He was my first boy-friend. My only boy-friend, really. We look happy don't we? Don't you think so?'

For several moments, Paul sat silent and uncomfortable under her scrutiny, taking a sip of coffee now and again. Her eyes glittered with tears or anger. She was by no means the mild, negative sort of person he'd imagined — when he'd bothered to imagine her at all.

At last he decided to fight back. 'I admire you,' he said quietly. 'I like a person with guts. I hope we can be friends later on.'

'Never,' she said, with a shake of her black hair.

He ignored the interruption. 'I admire someone with guts,' he said again. 'You remind me of my mother, you do, and I mean that as compliment because she's a bloody wonderful woman. When my father told my mother he was leaving her she pushed his best suit in the lavatory and pulled the chain on it. I like someone with fight in them. But I'm afraid you've come up against something you can't fight. On any reckoning, you have all the advantages. You're Gareth's wife, the mother of his children, you have youth and looks on your side — yes, you're a very good-looking young woman. On my side, nothing. Except Gareth's nature. And you can't fight against nature.'

'Go,' she said when she realised he'd finished. 'Go then. There's nothing more to say.'

And she stood up clenching her fists.

Paul knew he'd never be able to forget her.

Husband and wife accompanied him to the door, but neither he nor they said anything further.

He had no idea when he'd see Gareth again.

ELEVEN

Sally was in the shop by ten o'clock, and by eleven was heartily bored. Not a single customer had called.

Marian had said she was on no account to bother with any polishing or dusting — not that she would have, anyway — but what else was there to do? She buffed her nails, read the headlines in the previous day's *Telegraph*, examined herself, looking distant and calm, in a cloudy eighteenth century mirror, buffed her nails again.

She rummaged through Paul Dainton's desk, but found only V.A.T. accounts, bills and receipts. She opened one of his reference books and tried — and failed — to read an article about commodes. There was nothing worth looking at in the shop apart from a pair of huge Chinese vases, scarlet and gold, hideous enough to be a talking point, and a small, bronze, sharp-looking kingfisher which she turned over once or twice; nothing tempting enough to buy or even covet.

Then she saw on the back wall an old map of Pembrokeshire and was immediately seized with a longing to go again to the mountain where she'd been with Gerald Maitland a couple of days ago. She studied the map, but it meant little to her; she couldn't remember the names of any of the small villages they'd passed on their way. In spite of that, she'd like to try to find it again, she thought. She'd like to be there on her own. She'd felt a strange restlessness after returning to Marian's that evening, a tingling under the skin, rather like the beginning of an illness.

By this time it was a quarter to twelve. Should she leave? Why not? Who'd know or care if she closed the shop early?

With no further hesitation, she slipped out, locked the door and walked up the road to fetch Marian's car. It was a glorious day.

Of course she should have had a snack, or at least a cup of tea, before setting out. She should have changed her formal black and white, worn to impress all the customers who hadn't turned up, for something brief and cool. As soon as she was in the car, she felt hot, sticky and thirsty. Where was she rushing to like a mad thing? And why?

For a time she stuck to the main road, driving against a hopeless queue of traffic to the coast, then, to get away from the stream of cars, took a left turn along a minor road, then a right turn, she wasn't sure why. The sign-post at the first cross-roads she came to offered a jumble of consonants impossible to pronounce. Left again. She was in a foreign country.

The landscape, too, suddenly took on an air of mystery. A strange light fell on the small stunted trees and the gorse bushes and the melancholy hills. She was longing for a drink. She'd surely reach a pub before closing time. But there was no sign of a pub, nor houses either, only a farm or two in the distance and the empty road.

She hummed. She felt moderately cheerful. Driving was really rather pleasurable on deserted country roads. Marian would be at Paddington by this time or already on the tube to Alan's flat. (How could he bear to live in a basement flat in Finsbury?) They'd have a great deal to talk about. Perhaps some good would come of it.

In any case, she'd try not to despair. Not today. Today she'd try not to think about the way her life was running down, dwindling, declining...Stop. Stop. She'd concentrate on the road, on her hands on the wheel, on hedges and gates, sheep, clouds, leaves, shadows, all the patterns of colour and shapes. Blue and green and yellow and grey. Blue sky, green leaves, yellow sunshine, grey thoughts. Grey, grey, grey. It's over. Everything's over, everything that made life worthwhile. Stop.

A pub at last. A small white pub. Two fat farmers regarding her. A woman behind the bar. 'Are you lost, Miss?'

'No. No, thank you. A pint of cider, please. Do you have any sandwiches? Cheese? That will be fine. Thank you.'

Time passed. The farmers left. She sat on in the cool dark room.

'Are you all right, Miss? Only we're closing now, I'm afraid.'

'Yes, thank you. I'm feeling better now. It was good cider.'

Would you like to take the sandwiches with you, Miss? I'll fetch you a bag.'

'Thank you.'

And it was hotter than ever. And the road still winding uphill, but now she couldn't remember where she wanted to go, or why. Though it was still pretty enough. Blue, green, yellow, grey. Blue, green, yellow, grey.

This seemed to be it. Why had she said that? It was no different from any other turning, but the track led to a clump of stunted trees on the right which looked familiar.

She stopped the car and got out. She'd seen those trees before, of course she had. She'd arrived at the very spot she'd been to on Thursday with Gerald. He'd parked his car less than twenty yards away. She could see the outcrop of rocks where they'd sat for their picnic.

Yes, and she knew, now, why she'd had to come back. She wanted to think about those things Gerald had mentioned. They sounded feasible on this mountain, under this sky. This was holy ground, he'd said, holy to the Goddess who was worshipped here. Surely it was just possible, that sacred places, sacred stones, retained some vestiges of their former power? Wasn't it?

She started to walk towards the burial mound at the top of the hill. It was cooler now.

'What are you doing here?' she shouted at the young man at her feet.

She couldn't stop herself trembling with shock and indignation.

'Nothing,' he said angrily. 'I was lying here looking at the clouds that's all. Why didn't you look where you were going?'

'You were lying in wait for me,'

'Don't be so stupid. I've never seen you before in my life. I'm not waiting for anyone. I came up here to be by myself.'

'I'm sorry,' she said after a few moments. 'I'm sorry I shouted at you. I had such a fright.'

'Well, I'm sorry I frightened you. I certainly didn't mean to. You'd better sit down. You're white as a sheet. Aren't you well?'

'I'm all right now. I wasn't looking where I was going. I didn't even see this hollow. I didn't expect to see anyone here, that's all. '

'I've never seen anyone here before. People usually stick to the path on the other side. You still look as though you're going to faint. Put your head down between your knees.'

Sally did as he told her. She was feeling faint. She should have eaten something, she knew. 'What time is it?' she asked him.

'About four, I should think. Not much later.'

She looked at her watch. 'Ten past four,' she said. 'I didn't realise I'd been driving for so long.'

'You look better now. I'll be on my way. Leave you to yourself.'

He got up, turned towards her, nodding his head.

'No, don't go. I can give you a lift. Where do you want to go?'

'I've got a motor-bike, thanks.'

'I'm sorry I shouted at you. I was in a dream, that's all.'

'I had a shock too, I can tell you. I didn't see you come. You almost walked into me.'

She didn't want him to go. Suddenly the place was too lonely, almost frightening. 'Do you live round here?' she asked him.

'Used to. In a village over in that direction. Mile and a half in that direction. You could see the house except for those trees. I've moved now. Well, seven years ago.'

'Do you often come back? Do you often come up here?'

'Once in a while.'

'Do your parents still live here?'

'Yes.'

'I'm looking for somewhere to stay. Is there a pub around that does accommodation?' She was trying desperately to delay him.

'I don't know. It's caravans mostly, round here. Down by the river, anyway. There are several caravan parks. The pubs are mostly quite small. There's plenty of hotels on the coast, of course. Don't you like the sea?'

'Yes, I love it. Not that I know this coast. I've never been to Pembrokeshire before.'

'Where do you usually go?'

'I go abroad sometimes.'

'I'd like to go abroad. Some hopes.'

'This is quite as good. Better.'

'It's not bad in this sort of weather, but I can't say I'm over fond of it. Not this part, anyway.'

'You seemed pretty engrossed in the view.'

'I was just trying to think, really. I can't say I notice views much. Or mountains, for that matter. I just got on my bike and this is where I finished up.'

'It was a bit like that for me, too.'

It seemed very strange when she started to think about it. Did it mean anything? She started to tremble again. 'I've been ill,' she said.

'You don't look well.'

He sat down again, a little reluctantly. 'What's been the matter with you?' he asked. 'I don't like to leave you here on your own. Is it a nervous condition, or what?'

'It is, I suppose.'

'Well then, what you need is a bit of company. This is the worst sort of place for you, this is. Staying in a small pub around here would finish you off.'

He edged a little nearer to her. 'If I were you, I'd drive on to Tenby,' he said. 'There's some good hotels in Tenby. It's a nice town, lively. It would suit you. And the visitors are a very decent lot. You'd make friends in no time. You'd be taken out of yourself.'

He wondered whether to tell her that he worked in a hotel in Tenby, but decided against it.

'Would you like me to walk back with you as far as your car?' he said instead.

'Not yet. I haven't got my breath back yet.'

She sat, leaning her head on her raised knees, looking at him.

'Why have you come here on your own?' she asked. 'I'd have thought you'd be out with your girlfriend this afternoon.'

He made no response .

'Haven't you got a girl-friend?' she asked, undeterred by his silence.

'No.' He glowered at her.

'I'm sorry. Don't be annoyed. I don't mean to pry. You don't look happy, though. You're not happy are you?'

'No.'

'So why not tell me about it? We're strangers. It's easier to confide in a stranger.'

He suddenly relaxed. 'Like the Samaritans, ' he said. 'I've rung the Samaritans once or twice, if you want the truth. Half-a-dozen times more like. Well, that's what they're there for, isn't it? The one I have is called Joyce. She was the one who answered the first time I rang, and now I always ask for her. Joyce. I don' t know her second name. She's very sympathetic. Well, of course she is. She wouldn't do it otherwise, would she? Be a Samaritan, I mean. They don' t get paid, you know. Only she seems a wonderful person, really warm and understanding. And nothing seems to shock her, nothing.'

'Pretend I'm Joyce,' Sally said. She didn't at all want to be Joyce, but talking about her had brought the boy to life for the first time. At one point she'd thought he was going to smile.

'No,' he said. 'She's much older than you.'

'How do you know?'

'She sounds much older, anyway.'

'I'm Joyce. I followed you here. I wanted to see what you looked like. You see, I couldn't stop thinking about you.'

Again he almost smiled.

'You look just as I'd imagined,' she continued, 'A young Burton.'

He rejected the flattery with a dismissive jerk of the head.

'OK,' he said, 'If you're Joyce, help me. What am I going to do now? I've done what I told you I was going to do and I feel bloody rotten about it. Well, come on Joyce.'

'I mustn't advise you, I must only listen to you. Try to tell me why you feel rotten. Do you feel guilty?'

'Of course I feel guilty. I've told you and told you how guilty I feel.' Sally sighed. 'Everyone feels guilty. One should try not to. I think we have the right to do what we most want to do. We haven't got long'.

'Till when?'

'Till Doomsday.'

'Oh God, don't tell me you're another of these religious cranks.'

'I feel religious up here. I was born too late. I should have been a Priestess not a Samaritan. I could do you much more good if I were.'

'Don't start to preach religion to me, for God's sake. You'd really be wasting your time.'

'I'm not a patch on Joyce, am I?'

'No. She doesn't cry. She just says, "And what do you feel about that?" over and over again.'

'She sounds half-witted.'

'Don't cry. It's easy to cry, but it doesn't do a bit of good. Look, let's go for a walk. I'll take you to a place I know. It's only a pile of stones really, but everybody goes there. It's the remains of one of these ancient monuments or something.'

They walked along the side of the hill over the short, springy grass. The sky was darkening, but they hardly noticed it.

'I've left my wife,' he said, quietly and casually as they went.

'Your wife! Good Lord, you don't look old enough to have a wife.'

She looked at him as they walked. She'd thought he was twenty or twenty-one.

'I've got two kids as well,' he said.

'When did you leave her? Why?'

'I love someone else.' His voice softened. 'A man.'

'Oh!' she said. A round noise like a bullet.

'You're shocked, aren't you? Joyce wasn't shocked.'

'Of course I'm not shocked...What do you take me for?' She wanted to add something hurtful and witty.'Nowt as queer as folk,' would have done as a start, but his eyes were like a puppy's.

'The only thing is,' she said, after too long a pause, 'that you may be mistaken. Why did you get married if you're a homosexual?'

The sky above them suddenly shook.

'We'd better run to the car,' she said. 'Look at the sky.'

They started to run downhill.

'Hold my arm if you want to,' he said. 'What about taking your shoes off? You can't run in those heels. That's right. I'll carry them for you, You've got your bag.'

She let him go first whilst she ran and slid and slithered just behind him. Thunder growled in the distance.

The cloud broke when they were only a few yards away from the car, but the torrent of rain soaked them even in that short time. They shouted out with the force of it.

'The key, the key. Oh, now I can't see the lock.'

'Let me do it.'

They got in at last and shook themselves and laughed. The rain tumbled over the windows of the car like waves. They were under the sea.

'If only I had a towel.'

'You'll soon dry off . It's warm in here.'

'Is it? I can't stop shivering.'

'What a storm. I've never seen such rain. I'm lucky to be in here with you. I'd be sheltering under those trees, otherwise. Perhaps I'd have got struck by lightning.'

'Perhaps the car'll be struck by lightning.'

'No. Cars are safe.'

'When it's stopped a bit, I'll run you home. Did you say your parents live near here?'

'But I hardly ever go back there. Not now.'

'Why not?'

'I can't be bothered. I've grown away from them.'

'That sounds unkind.'

'Joyce would never say that.'

'She'd say. "And what do you feel you should do about that?" She's not going to help you much, believe me.'

'She already has. Put my jacket over your shoulders. You aren't half shivering.'

'I wonder if the car will start after this?'

'Yes, why not?'

'Do you know much about cars?'

'Not all that much. I've never owned one. But I'll stay with you till you get away, so don't worry. I can go and get someone — I know where there's a garage — I mean, if the worst comes to the worst. As long as my bike starts up. It should do.'

'I'm not mad about lightning, are you?'

'Yeh, I like it.'

'I've got some sandwiches. Would you like one? Cheese.'

'I'll have one if you will. It may stop you shivering.'

They ate the sandwiches. The bread was thick and fresh and the cheese neither too mild nor too strong.

They both began to feel more cheerful.

'If you're really sure you're a homosexual, then you must be doing the right thing,' Sally said, when she'd finished eating. 'I mean, in leaving your wife.'

'And kids. Two kids.'

'Even so, it's the right thing. You could never be a happy family, could you? Even if you stayed together. She wouldn't be happy for a start, if she's a normal woman. How old is she?'

'Twenty-five.'

'It would be better for her in the long run. She's young enough to get married again. She probably will in no time at all.'

'Oh God, I wish I thought so. It's not that I've ever been such a marvellous husband. I mean, I don't earn all that much. I work rotten hours, I'm a chef, see, assistant chef, work six nights a week. She doesn't have nights out, only when she goes to her parents or to Bingo, and we've only had one proper holiday in seven years. Only, to her, marriage is important. She's contented. I don't say she's happy, but I don't think she ever expected to be, not really happy, not the way I want to be. She just likes the comfortable routine of marriage. I think she even likes being hard-up, scraping and saving, managing the house-keeping, putting aside 50p's for the gas, the family allowance for the boys' clothes. She likes...all that.'

'And she doesn't mind having to do without love?'

He looked out at the rain. It was slackening off by this time. On the horizon, the sky was gleaming silver.

'Or she's never noticed,' he said at last, 'You see, I like her very much. She's a nice person. She's a good mother. Everybody likes her.

She gets on well with everybody. I'm usually able to be quite loving towards her.'

'But what about sex? Doesn't she mind doing without sex? Or would you rather not talk about that?'

'After the little one was born, two and a half years ago now, she's slept in the front bedroom with him, and I've slept in the small bedroom with the older boy. They keep each other awake if they're in the same room. It's quite a good arrangement.'

'And that's it?'

'I'm often late, see, when I work evenings, twelve and one when I get home. And that way I don't disturb her. And neither of us wants another baby. Well, we couldn't afford one anyway. So that's how it was. Only, it was wrong, somehow.'

'You were living a lie,' Sally said, italicising the words.

He glanced at her sharply, aware of the mockery in her voice.

'It's him I want to be with,' he said. 'And it's not just sex. He's interesting. He's fun to be with. My life is fuller. We're close in all sorts of ways. Oh yes, it's sex mostly, I'm sure. You see, I can't see him without wanting to touch him. I was never like that with my wife. Not even at the beginning.'

Sally felt rebuffed. 'I hope your wife will let you see the children from time to time,' she said stiffly.

'She probably won't. She's very bitter. And the courts won't help me much, will they? He's warned me about that. He's almost as upset as I am. He's fond of children. So it's all a bloody awful mess, isn't it? Christ, why did I do it? Get married, I mean.'

'Why did you come up here?' she asked, wanting to change the subject.

'I don't know. I told you. Everything just got too much for me. I just slammed the door, got on my bike and drove off. I thought I might be able to think more clearly up here, I suppose. It might have been that. If so, it was an instinct. I didn't think it out. What are you getting at? Oh, I know there's supposed to be some sort of magic about this place, but I've never believed in anything like that.'

'You haven't?'

'Good Lord, no.'

'But yet, this is where your instinct brought you. You might not believe in it, but the blood in your brain may carry some sort of signal, from people who believed in it very strongly.'

'You mean, something like tribal memory?'

'Something like that. I'm sure I've been affected by something like that.'

'Is that why you came up here, then?'

'Yes. I want something from this place. Power, I think. They say energy can't be destroyed. This mountain, its burial mounds — which were places of worship as well as burial — was a repository of energy. The rain's stopped. Look at those trees, the leaves are like gold in this light. You said you'd take me to see that chamber. Will you? Now?'

The power of the Goddess, Sally said to herself as she got out of the car.

A little hesitantly, he followed her.

TWELVE

'Alan, you must tell me what to do. Please.'

He was lying with his head between her breasts. She knew he was awake, but he refused to answer her, just grunted and pretended to be asleep. She pulled her hand out from somewhere under his body and looked at her watch.

'I've missed my train,' she said. 'I must phone Sally.'

For two hours she'd been someone else, someone she'd never come across before, and wouldn't have approved of if she had. What had happened? Making love, for her, had always been a pleasant but rather grave thing. Sometimes she'd welcomed Dickie's advances — though usually from tenderness rather than desire — sometimes tolerated them, but in either event had felt relaxed and pleased afterwards, as one did after taking exercise; swimming or a long walk. It had always signalled that the marriage was alive and well. Sex cemented a marriage. She'd read that somewhere — in fact almost everywhere — and was convinced that it was true: she'd seldom felt the symptoms of stress and frustration that others complained of.

With Alan, though, sex had seemed something altogether more positive; less a matter of cement than of renewal, regeneration.

She hadn't wanted it at all, certainly hadn't invited it in any way. When he'd insisted on helping her out of her wet dress, she'd squawked and gibbered enough, of course she had, and she'd never have allowed herself to be persuaded into the bedroom if it hadn't been for the acute embarrassment of finding herself — and him — half-naked at the kitchen window; and she at least ten pounds over-weight.

But it had been thrilling. Admittedly, there'd been years of abstinence behind it, but that in itself couldn't have accounted, surely, for all the fluttering and trembling she'd felt as soon as he'd started to touch her; her lips, let alone her breasts. Oh, and her breasts still ached as though they'd had little climaxes of their own. Also her throat. Her body seemed to have so many different parts. Its complexity amazed her.

106

There was no point at all in feeling embarrassed. Alan was obviously a very experienced man. She'd have to try to think of him as women were urged to think of their doctors during an intimate examination; it meant nothing to them; it was something they did every day. She tried to breathe deeply and calmly.

The bed was wide and smelt sweet and moist like kittens. Or a pine wood.

Only two hours. But she'd always remember it. Nothing comparable had ever happened to her. In two hours, pain had been healed and sorrow assuaged; she'd somehow been liberated from the past.

Steady on, she told herself. Don't, for God's sake, try to make a Big Thing out of this. It's a sexual encounter of a rather sordid kind, that's all. This man sprawled across me, his head even now burrowing further into my left arm-pit, is the husband of my dearest friend. And if her behaviour left something — or almost everything — to be desired, yet two wrongs don't make the position any better.

Once that's accepted, she told herself, one can also admit to a quite extraordinary degree of pleasure, even joy. She had had joy of him, she thought. What lovely lad most pleasured me, of all that with me lay. Lines of poetry suddenly took on substance. The shy, dark-haired man she'd known — and more or less ignored — for years, had become her lovely lad. Her nipples became hard again and there was a sucking tide in the sea of her body.

Oh, but he was lovely. She'd already got used to his changed appearance; he seemed, now, most familiar and dear. His hair, close to, was astonishingly beautiful, thick and shiny with an occasional pure white strand in the black. She shifted slightly in order to kiss it and as she did so, he stirred. 'Marian,' he said, and the surprise and delight in his voice melted her bones.

'I've missed my train,' she said again.

'Good,' he said. 'I'm glad.'

And then he said something else she must surely have misheard, because they weren't words she'd ever met with before; not spoken.

'What did you say?' she asked. Because, curiously enough, the mere idea of hearing the words were creating fresh little tremors and wavelets in her body, and when he pulled her on top of him and repeated the words into her ear, she started to moan again in the most shameless way, continuing at intervals for the next few minutes.

What a fool I am, she said to herself afterwards. I'm nearly forty-five and I've wasted my life.

'What are you thinking about?' Alan asked her. His voice was back to normal, pleasant and rather sad.

'I'm wishing I could stay here with you,' she said. It seemed like someone else talking. It was direct and clear. It was the truth. Had she ever spoken the truth before?

He didn't answer, but it didn't worry her. She felt like a tree or a hill, beyond having to think of consequences. She'd never felt so complete, so full of herself. Was this new self her real self? She'd always prided herself on knowing her limitations. As she'd readily accepted that she wasn't beautiful, though moderately easy on the eye, she'd also accepted that she wasn't passionate, sensuous, ardent, but all the same, loving and by no means frigid. Alan, though, had held up a mirror and shown her a completely new reflection. And she'd have to get used to it, she supposed.

They lay twined together, their bodies sweating under the cotton bedcover. The rain had stopped and then begun again a delicate, silver pattering. Traffic sounded in the distance, planes passed by from time to time, a fly buzzed on the window pane, a clock ticked. It was the same old world. Only she was different.

'Shall we go out for a meal?' Alan asked, when they were getting dressed. 'Or shall I cook you something here?'

'Oh dear, I shall have to phone Sally first. I'm so worried about missing the train.'

'Tell her I'll meet her in town sometime. That may get her off your back.'

He stood watching her lovely deep breasts being persuaded back into their pretty lace cages.

'It isn't me she wants, Marian,' he continued, after a few seconds. 'She just has this need to re-live the past. She can't let it go. Having the wronged husband around, helps to keep it alive.'

Marian fastened her bra for the second time. 'Or perhaps she loves you,' she said.

'I can't get through, Alan. The lines are down. There must have been storms everywhere. I'll have to try again later.'

'Don't look so worried, darling. You can't help Sally. Nobody can. Come and sit down. I've made some more tea.'

108

He patted the chair close to his and smiled. She sat down and took the cup of tea he passed her. The evening sun slanted into the kitchen through pink-tipped clouds. It was another lovely moment.

Alan ran his fingertips over her face. 'I've been half in love with you for twenty years,' he said. 'You must have known.'

'How could I have known? You were Sally's husband. I've never been perceptive. I don't see further than the end of my nose.'

'Lovely nose,' he said.

The kitchen was painted in strident colours; lime-green, peacock blue and blotting-paper pink. The round table was white with a swirling pattern of silver stars. I'll remember this, she thought. Such a young room. She sighed and stifled the thought of its young owner.

'We'll go to the new Italian restaurant in Camden,' Alan said. 'We can't spend the evening here. The sitting room's in such a mess, the paintwork not dry and the funiture all in one corner.'

'I'll have to find somewhere to stay tonight.'

He clutched her hands. 'But won't you stay here? You will, won't you? Why not? You can't run away now. I need you. I need you.'

She felt giddy. The kitchen's violent colours rose and dipped in front of her. Their eyes fluttered and closed. Their mouths met again, damp and warm.

'Well, if you're sure it's all right,' she said at last.

'I'm sure,' he said, his hand on her heart.

'When is you girlfriend coming back?' she asked then, needing to keep some sort of hold on reality.

'Not for another ten days.'

'Are you decorating the sitting-room as a surprise for her?'

He shrugged his shoulders. 'Or to pass the time.'

'What's her name?'

'Hannah.'

'Is that her picture in the hall?'

'Yes.'

'She looks nice.' And so young, she thought. Those wide-apart, candid eyes. That trusting smile.

'She is nice. But...young. Let's go out.'

The restaurant was full and noisy but they sat close together and held hands while they waited to be served. Alan had changed into a light-weight suit, but Marian had to make-do with describing her new honey-coloured dress of tussore silk and her rope of pearls. He said he had always thought of her as wonderfully voluptuous, but luckily his words were lost in a burst of laughter from the next table: she was feeling pale and languid and almost slim.

They ate and drank and gazed at each other.

'We must talk about Sally,' Marian said at last, when the restaurant was almost empty and fallen into melancholy after the babble and clatter and laughter, 'what shall I tell her tomorrow? What's going to become of her?'

For a moment she thought Alan wasn't going to answer; his face had hardened.

'I honestly don't know,' he said at last. 'She's seen two or three psychiatrists, but she won't do what they suggest; won't take any tablets, won't attend any therapy; finally they refuse to treat her. And she seemed to be getting worse instead of better. It reached a stage where I never knew if I'd be allowed to go out, even to work. Seeing me getting ready to leave the house seemed to be a signal for her to have one of her dreadful attacks of weeping.'

'I wish someone had let me know,' Marian said.

He took her hand again. 'Don't think I wasn't concerned about her, I was. But finally I decided that she'd have to pull herself together if I left her, and, honestly, she did improve up to a point. Virginia said she was almost back to normal when she was home for Easter — she had a new boyfriend and I suppose that helped. The next thing I hear, she's not even going to her classes, she's talking of resigning, perhaps she has. What do I do? There's nothing I can do.'

'You don' t think you could ever go back to her?'

'Look, I tried to make the break for years. Now that I've managed it, I wouldn't be fool enough to go back, would I?'

'I don't know. Since you did put up with such a lot...I don't know.'

'A week or two ago, I ran into Frances Somebody who's in the Vagabonds with her. Sally wasn't chosen as Rosalind for this year's Shakespeare production. That must have hit her very badly — she's had the lead for years, almost automatically. What's the answer? There isn't an answer. She can't get younger instead of older. She's getting older. Who isn't?' He seemed angry again.

'It's worse for her,' Marian said. 'Everyone's always made such a fuss about her looks.' She thought of a boy at University who used to lie down in her path whenever he saw her coming.

'And she's still good looking, God knows,' Alan said.'But she has the occasional set back now, and it's something she can't take. She's losing her power to dazzle — and it's the only thing that's ever meant anything to her.'

The waiter hovered around them, wanting them to go. Alan ordered more coffee.

'I'm being unfair,' he said then, in a low voice, 'I think Dickie meant a great deal to her.'

There were only two other people left in the restaurant. When the waiter returned, Alan and Marian seemed to be studying them intently. Alan ordered brandy.

'She thought he'd want to marry her when she became pregnant,' he said.

Marian stared at her coffee.

'But he didn't,' he continued. 'He just urged her to have an abortion. She wanted the baby quite badly. I told her to go ahead and have it. Oh, I may not have been very gracious or enthusiastic, but I think she knew I wouldn't have resented any baby of hers. Anyway, what's done is done. Christ, when I went to fetch her home from the clinic she was already regretting it.'

'No wonder she didn't come to see me when Dickie died. I thought it was because she felt awkward. So many people feel awkward and embarrassed, so afraid of saying the wrong thing that they prefer to stay away and say nothing. But she was suffering as much as I was, probably more.'

'Don't start to cry again, love. It doesn't do any good. Have some brandy.'

'He used to be so tense at times, but I always put it down to his work. Sometimes he'd be bad-tempered with the boys and I'd tell them it was because he was anxious about some particular patient or other. He should have told me. Somebody should have told me.'

'I don't think it would have helped much, Marian. As it was, you were spared a certain amount. You had enough to cope with when Dickie died.'

They grew silent. The other couple got up to leave and the waiter became restless again.

'I wish you didn't have to go back tomorrow,' Alan said. 'When will you come up again?'

'I won't be able to see you again, will I? Because of Hannah, I mean.'

'Hannah is a very temporary girl-friend, Marian. She comes and goes. With her rucksack and her guitar.'

His voice had softened.

'You love her,' she said. Before she could stop herself.

'Do I? Yes, of course I do. Yes. It's a ripple on the water, though, that sort of love. One wants....well....depth, I suppose.'

'Drop me a line when she next goes.' (He won't of course, she said to herself, but the possibility that he may will keep me going for a while.)

'I will. Oh, I will.' His eyes, seeking out hers were dark and unsmiling.

Marian's legs felt weak as she got up from the table. She tried to breathe slowly, tried to look her age, and kind and gentle and of sufficient depth.

THIRTEEN

Five o'clock and still no sign of Paul. Mrs Dainton dragged herself out into the kitchen to make a pot of tea.

She turned on the radio, but as usual it disappointed; opera, gardening questions (slugs) and a woman talking about things to make with silver wire.

'Silver wah?' Mrs Dainton said indignantly, deciding yet again on her own company.

Getting even with him, she said, as she poured herself a cup of well-brewed, blackish tea. That's where I'd got to, I think. Well, he started wanting a bit, didn't he. Elspeth was more interested in the house than in him. She shampooed the wall-to-wall dove-grey carpets every week, polished the furniture and the silver and the brass, washed blankets and curtains and cleaned all the windows in and out. It was when he noticed her cleaning the lavatory every time he had a pee that he realised she was not exactly normal and started hankering after the comfortable squalor of life with me. Also, she had very little conversation and what she had was refined.

So he started spending Wednesday nights with me, telling her he was having to stay over-night in Wolverhampton. Every Wednesday night for how many years was it? At least five. From '59 to '64, I think it was. It became the highlight of the week for me, only of course I didn' t let on. He pleaded for an extra night. I've got a hell of a lot of business in Wolverhampton, I really should give it two nights. But I wouldn't have that, no thanks. Before I knew where I was I'd be cooking for him again and washing his socks. I wasn't his wife, so I wanted to be treated right. I'd have insisted on a night in a posh hotel every week, except it would have taken too much organization.

How old was Paul at this time? Well, he'd be seven in '59. I've got a picture of him somewhere. He was almost normal-looking by that time. He didn't like school too much, but who does, and I was always confident he'd learn to read eventually, and of course he did, and whatever else he got up to wasn't found out. He got his O-levels, quite a string of them, and he wasn't expelled till his second year in the Sixth...Oh, but I'm running ahead of myself. Where was I? 1959,

113

Paul around seven, the others teenagers, and Eleanor in particular, needing a firm hand, she was far too like me for my peace of mind.

He was earning plenty of money by this time, Robbie was, and he gave me a good share of it. That was only fair — and, of course, he knew what I'd do if he didn't. We had no illusions about each other. We weren't in love, whatever that means, didn't even pretend to be. The only time I wore rose-coloured spectacles was when he'd given me a black eye. All we had between us was Wolverhampton, really. Well, I've got nothing against it. Specially when you can have champagne with it. And be in no danger of unwanted pregnancies.

Of course, none of the children ever found out I was having it off with their father. They'd have been really shocked. He'd come in about seven o'clock on the Wednesday evening — he didn't miss that day's work, though he generally took the morning off next day — and he'd help the kids with their homework till they went to bed. He was dead keen on them doing well at school. Maths was his great love, specially geometry. He'd work out those theorems as though they were the fount of all knowledge. They teach you to think, he'd say when I mocked him. Hah. He never learnt to think or he'd have left me alone.

And there she was, Elspeth, giving coffee-mornings in her lovely sterile house, *in aid of the blind*; that killed me, that did, and cleaning and polishing after them in the afternoons. And there was I, wicked Alice, traipsing about in my tarty clothes and my fur coat, watching her money — it was her business he was running — piling up nicely in my bank account.

Do you know, she thinks you must have a lover, the Rat told me one Wednesday night. She wonders whether I need pay you so much maintenance.

What did you say?

Don't be so bloody stupid, I said. A lover? Her? That ravaged old bag?

Men are easily deceived, she said. Oh, the way she minces about on those five-inch heels, her breasts up to her chin. She is a common piece.

How can I get at her? I shouted, almost leaping out of bed. How can I humiliate her? I'm afraid I'll have to let her know how her nasty black rat is behaving when he's out of her sight.

That would be the end of everything, my girl. Don't forget who's paying the piper. Let her say what she likes as long as she never finds out. Calm down now, that's it, that's it, that's it.

The storm interrupted her memories.
  She enjoyed its violence and intensity, feeling herself a part of it.
When she pointed her finger, the lightning lashed across the sky. With
her other hand she brought in the thunder. It was better than Bee-
thoven. She'd always loved a good storm.

When Paul came in he was alarmed by the demonic look on her face.

What the hell was wrong with Paul, she wondered. He'd come in
with his tail between his legs. Something wrong — or nothing. He
worried about nothing; little bills, little losses, little failures. He
couldn't think big, that was his trouble. He'd be satisfied to live in
this dreary flat over the shop for ever.
  Now he was fussing over her tea. She didn't want anything else to
eat. Just a piece of bread and butter and a slice of cheese, she'd said.
Why bother with cooking. He needed more than that, he'd replied.
He'd grill a couple of chicken pieces and make a salad.
  He told her nothing about his day. He'd helped her back to her
chair in the sitting-room and asked about Miss Morris, how she was
and how long she'd stayed. 'How was the plaice?' he'd asked, then.
  'A bit on the dry side,' she'd told him. 'Probably re-cooked. They
cook the pieces before the shop opens, then, when there's an order,
plunge them back into the frier for another couple of minutes. Same
with the chips. Dries them up. That's why you have to be so liberal
with the vinegar. And vinegar sours the blood.'
  He wasn't listening to her, she could tell.
  'What did you have for lunch?'
  'I didn't have any.'
  She clicked her tongue at him. 'No wonder you look done-in. Over
forty, you need to look after yourself. You're not a boy now, you
know. Have a glass of sherry.'
  'You know I hate the stuff...Can I get you some?'
  'I think I'd rather a Mackeson's. You should have one as well. So
should Miss Morris, but she won't listen. "What you need, Miss
Morris," I told her, "is a glass of Mackeson's every day. Far better for

you than poetry." Poetry! They have such notions, don't they, these old virgins? She told me today that she had a fiancé killed in the war. She never had a fiancé, believe you me. Has she ever mentioned any fiancé to you?'

'I don't plague her with questions like you do.'

He went into the kitchen. She could hear him clattering about, pleased to be out of her way.

It was costing Paul a considerable effort to remain even moderately civil to his mother.

Gareth hadn't turned up at the Regal Hotel where he was to have been in charge of the lunch-time grills. He hadn't even phoned, according to the manager, which was the limit, since there was no-one to stand in for him except for Max, who'd had no experience to speak of.

So he'd walked about all afternoon, going to all the places where they'd previously met, his mind full of misgivings and panic. He'd had to start back at five because of his mother, but first he'd gone back to the hotel — he'd surely turn up for dinner, Saturday night dinner being the busiest meal of the week — and left a desperate note for him. 'Please ring me. Please. I'm going out of my mind.'

What had happened to him? Had Susan managed to win him back? She was a formidable opponent, there was no doubt about that. He'd always imagined an insignificant little woman, but she was tough as steel. 'I'm the weak one, Gareth,' Paul cried out to him in the kitchen. 'I'm the one who needs you.'

'What's that you say? Speak up Paul. How can I hear you if you keep the door closed?'

When the meal was ready and the table laid, he switched on the television.

It's only so that he needn't talk to me, his mother said to herself. He doesn't like 'Jim'll Fix It.' Nobody does. Television is only popular because it means people don't have to talk to one another.

'There's a good film after this,' he said.

'Yes,' she said, very sweetly. 'Then there's a comedy show, and then the news. I'm going to have a splendid evening. What about you? I suppose you'll be going out as soon as you've washed up.'

He didn't answer her.

She watched his eyes move to the telephone, squatting dumb as a toad on the table in the hall.

She felt sorry for him, too.

He got ready to go out soon after seven. There'd been no phone call.

'You'll be all right? I've left your cocoa ready on the tray. You'll only have to boil the kettle.'

'I'll be all right.'

'Take care with it, won't you. Don't scald yourself as you did last year.'

'Oh, go out. Stop fussing over me. Enjoy yourself.'

'Goodnight then, Mum. Gareth may call to see you tomorrow. I'll invite him to tea.'

'That'll be nice, dear.'

And they went on for five years, those Wednesdays. What we got up to! Well, I suppose we weren't the first. Funny how I got to like it so much though, after years of being frigid, very near. I'd come to terms with him, I suppose, after years of fighting him all the way.

He was too sure of himself, that was part of the trouble, all along. Both of us wanting to be top dog.

We still fought — oh, it was war often enough — but we made peace after, and we'd never been able to before. Every so often I thought I was in love with him, but God damn it, I thought, I'm not going to make a fool of myself now. Not at my age.

Anyway, Eleanor left school and got herself a job in a solicitor's office. It was a wonderful start, he said. He was very proud of her. I wanted her to do something a bit more lively, like being a police-woman, she'd always enjoyed shouting at people — and she still does, come to that — but they took no notice of me.

And she'd got engaged to the junior partner in the firm and wanted to get married right away. I was against it, of course. She'd had no fun out of life. But he thought this fellow was such a bloody catch, this long-faced wimp with his public-school accent. Actually. I say. Look here, old chap. Silver wah. Silver wah. Silver wah. Nobody called Selwyn could be any good.

For weeks we were at loggerheads. When he called on a Wednesday evening, I ranted and raved and wouldn't let him stay the night.

I shouted and screamed at Eleanor too, begging her to wait a year or even six months, before committing herself to the first man who'd noticed her, but of course I couldn't shift her, either.

He and Elspeth were planning a big church wedding with a reception at The Little Foxes Country Club after.

I think they all hoped I was going to be too angry to turn up, but ducking out of something was never my style.

I bought a very elegant dress and jacket, a clinging crepe affair in two shades of grey, and a gorgeous white hat — kept the bills for him, of course — and had my hair cut and styled in the West End, in one of those places where every Cockney mother's son is called Patrice or Jean-Paul.

Came the day, I played it very dignified and wistful, the deserted wife with her three children, Richard, Laura and Paul. And he (the Rat) fell for it like the sucker he was.

'She must be in the photographs,' he said outside the church. And so there I am on his arm — mother of the bride, just off centre-stage — and he whispering to me, 'I'm mad about you, I'm mad about you. Please let's make it up.'

'Come tonight,' I said, in between shots. 'I'll be feeling strange without Eleanor.' (You know that feeling when a toothache stops.)

'She's giving a bloody party tonight, for all the bloody Bradley clan.'

'I'm giving a party too,' I said. 'and it's going to be one of those all-night affairs.'

I was on my own, Paul in bed, Richard and Laura still at the Country Club, when he came round.

'Doesn't Elspeth mind your leaving her party?' I cooed.

'I'm going to crush every bone in your body,' he said, hoisting me over his shoulder and carrying me upstairs as though I was the bride.

I felt like the bride. I wanted it as much as he did that night. Wanted to be hurt, wanted everything.

And that was the night he had a heart attack and died.

I'll have to have another look at that photograph. Eleanor's wedding. Where we look so happy, so united. Mother and father of the bride after twenty idyllic years, that's what we look like. I'm mad about you, he was saying with his hand on my arse.

The strange thing, the totally uncharacteristic thing, was that when the doctor came, I was crying and saying things like, I hope his wife won't need to know he was with me, and, I don't want to cause any trouble. I don't want her to be hurt.

Which only goes to show what a state I was in.

I suppose I loved him all the bloody time, bloody rat that he was. It must have been something like that, God damn it. The storm's cleared my bloody skull. Even going out with all those other men during the war — it was only to feel nearer him really. Being with someone else filled up his absence. Anyone was more like him than no-one at all. All my life in love with one rotten man, God damn it. How could he leave me for that soulless bitch?

'Oh, my dear Mrs Dainton. You're in pain. I've caught you at a bad moment. Let me fetch you something. Some disprin? A drop of brandy?'

She looked at Gerald Maitland as though trying to place him.

'I'm a bit better now,' she said at last. 'This bloody arthritis. You know how it gets me sometimes. Getting better now, thank the Lord. You could get me a drop of sherry, though, if you'll join me. The bottle's over on the trolley. I think you'll find some glasses there as well.'

'Yes. Yes. Yes. Here we are.'

In the street below, Mrs Dainton happened to see the young woman from the flat across the road, leaving for her Saturday night at the pub. Her pink dress was tight across her round breasts, her bold, wide mouth a slash of cherry-red. What made her look up and wave? Mrs Dainton waved back and tried to mouth a vital message through the window. Give it to them. Don't give a sucker an even break. Don't give anyone an even break. Fight back. Don't give in... careered through her mind, but all she managed to say was 'Cheers'.

And 'Cheers', she said to Gerald Maitland when he brought her a glass of sherry, filled to the brim and soon running over on to the table at her side.

'I'm glad I came,' he said, relieved to see her looking so much more her usual self.

He pulled up a chair and took a sip of his sherry.

'Paul called by on his way to Tenby. He said you seemed a bit low. It was probably the storm, don't you think? We certainly get storms in this part of the world.'

'Did Paul ask you to call?'

'He dropped the hint, as you might say. And I took it up and asked him for the key. I always enjoy a spot of company on a Saturday night.'

Gerald Maitland pressed his palms together, almost as though he were praying. The sight of Alice Dainton in tears had completely unnerved him, but the sherry, sticky and sweet though it was, was beginning to revive him.

'Marian should be back soon,' he said. 'I suppose her friend's going to meet her. I tried to ring her to check on it, but all the lines are down.'

'Are they? That explains it. Paul was expecting a call,' Mrs Dainton said, almost to herself.

'And she wasn't in the house when I came by. I rang the bell, but there was no reply.'

'She's a beautiful woman, isn't she? Mrs Rushton?'

Gerald Maitland looked about him wildly. 'Mrs Rushton? Oh yes, I suppose she is. Oh yes.' He pressed his palms together again.

'But what's worrying her? What makes her so...strange? There's a mystery there somewhere. Never mind. She's no stranger than all the rest of us, perhaps. I mustn't pry.'

'You really are under the weather, aren't you, Mrs Dainton? Shall I fetch someone? Dr Ansell?'

'No. Just sit for a while and keep me company. I'm a lonely old woman and perhaps I'm not so wicked as I've always tried to make out. I've tried hard to shock people, but perhaps it's because I can't bear to be pitied.'

'There's nothing wrong with being proud. It's a virtue, in my opinion. I get impatient with people who're always feeling sorry for themselves, behaving as though they're having to bear all the ills of the world. We all have our share, if you ask me. The turmoil of things never stops.'

'You're right. I know I never had an easy life.'

'But I'm sure you made the best of it.'

'I knew how to fight back.'

'Cheers!' they said to each other again, sipping their drinks.

But Gerald Maitland, that evening, couldn't stop himself thinking about his wife, Marjorie, who hadn't known how to fight back; of how badly he'd treated her, of how guilty he'd felt when she'd died

— and after no illness to speak of.

He'd always loved her, even when he was putting all his time and energy into his work, even when he was most busily being unfaithful to her. They'd never quarrelled. Not once in thirty years.

They'd been happy, surely.

How pretty she was when they were first married, so pale and fair and delicate. Her hands were white and soft, quite boneless they seemed, and her wrists so small. She used to dress so daintily, pearl earrings, lace collars and the prettiest little pointed shoes. At first, he'd tried to take her out with him on field-trips, but she was nothing of a walker, and how she hated the wind, or any weather to speak of.

'You don't have children?' Mrs Dainton asked him. She knew he didn't.

'No. It was a great disappointment to us. My wife was rather frail. She had a miscarriage once, I nearly lost her. I wouldn't let her risk anything after that.'

He sighed and they drifted into another silence.

'What about some more sherry?' Mrs Dainton asked.

'I will if you will,'

'By all means. Cheers!'

It was past eleven and there was still no sign of Paul. Gerald Maitland went to the window, lifted the curtain and looked out.

There was no-one in the street. The sky was pale and cloudless, the hills a purple smudge in the distance.

I treated her like a princess, he told himself.

All the mornings he had taken his breakfast alone and hurried out of the house without waking her, phoning her later from college to wish her a good morning. 'How are you, dear? Are you feeling any stronger today? I'm so glad. Would it be better if I had my meal in town before coming home? Of course I don't mind if it makes it easier for you. Will Mrs Tims make you some lunch? Why not ask her to come again tomorow? Of course we can afford it, Anything to help you. Take care. I love you.'

And he would have another carefree evening with Mary Nelson or Pamela Carter or...

'I'm sorry I'm late, dear. I thought you'd have gone to bed. I had dinner with Geoffrey King and he wanted me to go back to his flat afterwards to cast an eye on his thesis. He's got some interesting theories and I didn't feel I should throw over the chance of keeping up with them. It's surprising how often an idea, even in quite a different field of research, will trigger off something in one's own.

Why don't you go up to bed now? Yes, I really ought to work for another hour or so before I turn in. Look, why don't I spend the night in the spare room? Of course I don't mind if it means a better night's sleep for you. Good night, my love. I've thought about you all day.'

The day she died was not much different from any other day. Except that she had called to him as he was creeping past her bedroom door from the bathroom.

'Gerald.'

'Good morning, my love. I hope I didn't wake you.'

'I've been awake quite a while.'

'Then can I get you a cup of tea?'

'Would you? I know you haven't much time, but I'd be very grateful.'

'Of course.'

He'd set out a breakfast tray; a pot of tea, a small jug of milk, two slices of the thinest bread and butter, marmalade, and taken it up to her.

'I could do this every morning, you know.'

She'd smiled at him, no other reply.

'Shall I pour you a cup of tea?'

'Please.' (He'd been surprised at that).

He'd looked at her carefully: did her skin have a slightly bluish tint?

'We'll have to take a little holiday,' he'd said. 'I'll ring that hotel in the New Forest and fix it up.'

She'd smiled again and lifted the cup to her lips.

'I must go now. I'll phone you later.'

He'd phoned at ten o'clock. She'd told him she felt a little stronger, but intended having a day in bed.

'Good. Has Mrs Tims arrived?'

'Yes, she came half an hour ago.'

'Tell her not to bother with a meal for me. I'll have it here.'

'Don't be late, dear.'

As he put the phone down, he realised that it was the first time she'd ever asked him not to be late. Odd, he'd thought, before his mind had reverted to other things; to the article he was writing for an American scientific journal, to the television programme he'd agreed to appear on, to the television presenter's assistant he was taking out to dinner for the second time that week.

He'd managed to get the nine-thirteen train home and discovered that she had died earlier in the evening.

(Peacefully at her home in South Pembrokeshire, Marjorie (née Howard) beloved wife of Gerald Maitland, after a short illness bravely borne. Blessed are the pure in heart.)

'Of course you feel guilty,' Dr Ansell had told him. 'The next of kin always does. Blaming oneself for what one did or didn't do, for what one should have noticed, but didn't, for what one could have said but left unsaid, is the commonest form of grief. It's counter-productive though,' he'd said in a kindlier voice. 'Have a stiff whisky and try to immerse yourself in work, that's the best way to get through the next few days. By the way, my wife and I did enjoy your spot on that Sunday night programme the other week. Very good. Very good.'

Mrs Tims wasn't so sympathetic.

Early the next morning, she'd turned up, tight-lipped and dour, to give in her notice.

'But I shall need you more than ever now,' he'd been foolish enough to say. 'I mustn't get behind with my work.'

That had done it. He'd had to try not to listen to the flood of abuse which had followed. Unfeeling, selfish, pompous, unworthy, false, inhuman, cruel, were some of the things she'd called him.

When she had quite finished, she had demanded the money she was owed and a fur coat she'd been promised.

He'd paid her the exact sum of money she'd mentioned — not a penny more — and had indignantly refused her anything else.

As though prepared for this, she'd pushed a folded sheet of paper at him. On it was written: Mrs Doris Tims is to have my silver fox coat. Marjorie Maitland.

'When did she write this? he'd asked her, trying to keep his voice steady.

'In the spring when she was so ill.'

He'd felt himself begin to sweat. He hadn't been aware of any particularly serious illness during the spring, or indeed at any other time.

'Go up to fetch it,' he'd managed to say.

'I'll never go into that room again. Never.'

'Then I'll let you have it before the end of the week.'
'You'd better.'

Usually he managed to keep his mind occupied and under control, so that the unbearable memories were smothered before they could rise to possess it. The storm, though, seemed to have unleashed all the hell hounds.

I worshipped her, he told himself. We never had a quarrel in thirty years.

That evening, the words, usually potent, settled on his heart like lead. Like lies.

And then he remembered a particular afternoon — and not long before her death — when there'd seemed great sweetness and solace in their flawed relationship.

It was a pale gold day in early summer. He'd taken her for a drive in the hills and the air was so balmy that he'd persuaded her to venture out of the car and had settled her on the sun-bed he'd brought with him, and they'd had their flask of tea out of doors. He'd intended to take a walk to the top of the mountain, but the day was so lovely, so scented and still, the larks so exuberant, that he'd stayed sitting on a rug at her side all through the humming after- noon and well into the evening.

And when at last he'd made a move to go, she'd touched his arm and whispered, 'I'm sorry.'

'What about, my love?' he'd said —'What about? What can you mean? You've always been a perfect wife. I'm the one who should apologise, not you.'

That afternoon there'd been an intimacy between them deeper than the intimacy of sex, deeper than words could match.

The hour became her husband and my bride, he whispered to the night.

He imagined Foel Graig in the summer darkness, the full moon clear as glass, the breeze lifting the heather so that the great stone was like a ship on an ocean.

And moving at a dizzying speed as the earth moved round the sun.

And a man's lifetime a grain of sand in the wake of the mighty stars.

'I can't hear you,' Alice Dainton said, wondering at his gaunt, hunted look.

FOURTEEN

I still can't get a reply,' Marian said. 'It's ringing now but nobody's answering. Where *is* Sally?'

Alan was getting breakfast. He was cutting grapefruit, making toast. The table was prettily laid. It could have been such a happy morning. Except that she had to leave for the station in less than an hour.

'I'll ring Gerald,' she said. 'Gerald Maitland, my next-door-neighbour. He may know something.'

'Come and have some breakfast first. Try to relax.'

He came to fetch her and led her to the table. 'This has been such a wonderful week-end,' he said. 'I'll look back at it with such pleasure and gratitude. You're so lovely, so tender and generous. I've never done anything to deserve you, but my God, I appreciate my good fortune.'

He's making speeches, Marian thought, panic rising to her throat. He's making all the right, pretty noises and then he's going to put me on the train and let me go and I'll never see him again. This is a modern love-affair. This is an enriching experience, this is. Even if it leaves me bruised and scarred, I must pretend it's so worth-while and enriching and such fun.

'This is such fun,' she said, to see how it sounded.

For once, she wasn't hungry. She took a small piece of toast and wondered if she could manage to eat it.

He put his hand over hers. 'It's hell,' he said. 'I hate myself. How could I have been so careless? I've ruined all your memories. No wonder you look so stricken.'

'You only told me the truth — something I should have already known. I'll soon come to terms with it. It hasn't really changed anything. Dickie loved me and the boys, nothing can change that. I'm desperately sorry he had such a tormented time, but I have to try to put it out of my mind. I can't change it, however much I worry about it.'

Life will soon be bowling along again, she thought; boring and uneventful. How could I have thought I was even reasonably happy?

However much she chewed the toast, she couldn't seem to swallow it. She took a sip of coffee and immediately felt sick.

'I can't eat in the morning,' she said, laying down her cup.

'But you used to have a wonderful appetite. I have such a vivid memory of you in Provençe, spreading butter on a hot bagette and biting into it with rapture in your eyes. Can't we go back there? Just the two of us?'

'It would be lovely. But it won't happen.'

'Why not? Why shouldn't it happen? What's to prevent it? We're consenting and responsible adults aren't we? We can do what we like. Oh darling, we'd be so happy.'

He took her hand and kissed it.

'Come on, I'll feed you,' he said then. 'You're too upset to eat. I'll help you.'

With whole-minded concentration he scooped up small pieces of grapefruit and raised the spoon to her mouth. She could remember when he'd fed Virginia — and Tim, too — in the same absorbed way. How could she have been so unaware of him at that time?

'I can't,' she said, laughing and spluttering.

'All right. You needn't eat any more. At least you look happier.'

'I am happier. Thank you.'

She watched him finishing his breakfast. She felt ill with love.

'Why don't we go back to bed with the Sunday papers?' he asked. 'Wouldn't that be a nice idea?'

'I have to catch the 11.15 train,' she said.

'Bad news, I'm alraid,' were Gerald's opening words when she managed to contact him.

'Oh God, what now?'

Gerald needed no prompting. 'Such a frightful storm...didn't worry too much last night...called in about eleven thirty, but there was no reply...the car not in the garage...Miss Morris said the shop was already closed when she called to take Mrs Dainton some lunch...and if Elsie Lewis at the Greengrocers hadn't been in, goodness knows what....'

Marian couldn't make out what he was talking about.

'Are the boys all right?' she asked him.

'The boys? Marian, I've heard nothing about them. Why shouldn't they be all right?'

'What's happened to the boys?' Alan asked.

Marian put her hand over the mouth-piece. 'They seem to be all right,' she said.

She turned her attention back to Gerald. She spoke loudly and distinctly. 'Gerald, could you please give Sally a message from me. The phone at the cottage still seems out of order.'

'Sally's disappeared, Marian. What do you think I've been trying to tell you? No-one's seen her since yesterday morning. We don't know what to do. Where are you? When will you be back?'

'This afternoon. Don't worry, Gerald. Sally's never liked storms. She probably went to stay in a hotel somewhere, so that she wouldn't be on her own. Don't worry about her. She'll turn up. And when she does, will you please tell her I was held up by the storm. And don't forget to ask her to meet my train. At four thirty. I'll see you this evening, Gerald.'

She put the phone down .

'I've got to catch that train,' she said. 'Gerald's terribly worried about Sally. No-one has seen her since yesterday morning. Where ever do you think she can have got to?'

'I'll get the car,' Alan said, his eyes suddenly blank. 'Though I'm sure she's all right. She makes a habit of causing trouble.'

When he'd gone, slamming the door behind him, Marian stood in the tiny hallway looking round her. I've been so happy here, she said to herself. Or do I mean unhappy? Anyway, alive. Quite unlike my normal state.

She studied Hannah's photograph. What a friendly, down-to-earth girl she looked. Dear Hannah, I did like your bright little kitchen — and your great wide bed. If ever you hear about me, please believe that I came here quite innocently and left broken-hearted.

Oh, don't be so maudlin, she told herself. People are forever sleeping with people these days without making a great song and dance about it. It's not much more than a handshake, really. In Victorian times, people swooned over a kiss and thought that love conquered all and made the world go round, but now we know it's only a wholesome, health-giving experience like jogging and bran. She dried her eyes.

'Are you ready?' Alan asked.

'Yes thank you. I didn't have much packing.' (She hoped she wasn't blushing. She'd never slept naked before, nor cleaned her teeth with someone else's toothbrush.)

'I wish you didn't have to go.'

'So do I.' Hah. How cool that sounded. It was easy.

In the car, she got a bit emotional again.

'Are you thinking about Dickie?' Alan asked her.

It seemed easier to agree than to confess to her true state of mind which was, after all, a shock even to herself.

'Did you know that Dickie wrote poetry?' she asked him. It was something that had always impressed and surprised her.

Nothing about Dickie impressed or surprised Alan. 'Was it any good?' he asked sourly.

'I thought so. Unfortunately, I can't come across any of it, though I've searched through everything. I'd like to have been able to show some of it to the boys.'

'Are they into poetry?' Please let her talk about the boys, he thought. That, I could bear.

' "A moth is like a little white flower flying," that's about the only bit I can remember. "And something something something far away. But the day is dying, dying. And neither the thrush nor I can make it stay." '

Alan said nothing. He felt more jealous of Dickie's rotten poetry — or at least of the fact that Marian was crying over it — than he'd ever felt of his other undoubted gifts.

'Sounds a bit Tennysonian,' he said at last, since she seemed to be expecting some comment.

She wouldn't know how much he loathed Tennyson, his O-level poet. Morte d'Arthur and The Lady of Shalott made him feel almost reconciled to the rubbish Virginia's boy-friend wrote.

'Virginia's boy-friend writes poetry,' he said. 'That is, when he's not painting very large paintings. Guess who's the only person who's ever actually bought one of his paintings? That's right. It hangs in the passage outside my office. When I occasionally regret the good money I spent on it, I remind myself of the pleasure I'll get heaving it on to a bonfire when he eventually tires of Virginia.'

'Will he tire of Virginia? How do you know he will? You said he was very fond of her. Laughed off Sally's advances, you said.'

'That was last summer.'

'Perhaps she'll tire of him.' When she meets Tim again, she thought.

'No, I'm afraid Virginia's the faithful type, like me.'

He felt almost brutal 'I do hope you're not going to miss your train,' he said coldly, when they were held up at the lights for the third or fourth time.

'So do I.'

'You needn't stay,' she said a little later when they'd arrived at the station with almost ten minutes to spare.

'I may as well.' Bored. 'I've got nothing else to do. Shall l get you a coffee?'

'No thank you. I think the train's in.'

They walked on to the platform.

She could feel a tear crawl down her cheek and then another, but she shook them away. What had happened to the closeness between them?

The carriages were all full. They had to walk the length of the platform before they saw any empty seats.

As she got on the train, he suddenly relented. 'I'll come down to see you,' he said. 'Does the invitation still stand?'

'Of course. Any time. You've got my telephone number?' She clutched his hands.

'Don't worry about Sally. You don't owe her a thing.'

He kissed her through the open window and the train pulled away.

She'd managed to get a table with only one other person, a middle-aged woman, sitting in the window seat opposite her.

She sat back and looked at herself in her handbag mirror. To her surprise, she looked exactly the same as before. A shiny nose, but apart from that, the same healthy, olive-skinned, placid-looking, heart-whole woman. She snapped her bag shut and closed her eyes.

She felt another person. What had happened to her? She'd always been ready to judge people who snatched greedily at love without letting anyone or anything stand in their way: she had succumbed to temptation without a thought, let alone a fight. It had seemed the most right and natural thing in the world.

She thought of her mother who hadn't been able to enjoy a book or film which had in it any reference to adultery. What would she think of her? She wondered about her parents' marriage . They had seemed contented. Had they experienced joy in each other? Her mother had been very miserable when her father died; had shrunk into herself, becoming slower and more deaf, and was dead within a year. She used to talk a great deal about the war, what a dreadful ordeal her father's absence had been. Perhaps she'd felt as I feel now, Marian thought; all the nerves of my body quivering and aching like little broken things.

She wondered if Alan was missing her. He liked her well enough, there was no doubt about that. He'd remembered so many things about her, things she herself had forgotten; a long white party dress she'd had twenty years ago, a bright green cotton beach coat she used to wear in Provençe when they had breakfast on the terrace, a large straw hat with trailing ribbons.

He even remembered the rhymes she used to recite to the children. 'Star light. Star bright. First star you see tonight. I wish you would, I wish you might, Grant the wish I wish tonight.'

He'd recited that to her as they'd stood together in the cool glassy evening after the storm — was it only last night? He said he remembered her voice too, the whispery, bedtime voice she used when she read to the children. 'You were always so lovely, so dependable and kind,' he'd said. 'I often used to think about you. I've been half in love with you for years. I always expected to find you again one day.'

'I've found you.' That's what he'd said last night, or rather this morning, before they'd finally drifted off to sleep. 'I've found you.'

It was so moving; comforting and thrilling at the same time. She made herself think about Hannah, a slip of a girl, young enough to be her daughter. 'She comes and goes,' he'd said,' with her rucksack and her guitar.' And his voice had been loving and sad. She made herself think of Hannah's return in just over a week's time, of him whispering 'I've found you,' to her as they lay nuzzling together like two puppies on the bed which was so wide that there was no space for anything else in the room.

Would he ever come down to see her? Would she ever have another day — and a night — so lovely and so blessed? Love-making could be anything in the world, it seemed to her; wild, urgent, insistent, hard, dreamy, tender. Before, it had always seemed only one thing, a thing she couldn't now find a word for, except perhaps, connubial.

But how could she expect to be even a tiny part of his life? He already had a wife and a girl-friend.

All the same, he'd seemed to need her, last night.

His face was suddenly before her. She'd never really taken notice

131

of it before, in all the years she'd known him. Perhaps she'd always been too shy. But last night and during the morning, at the breakfast table, in the car, at the station, it had seemed beautiful; eager, secret, full of complexity, a face you would never tire of. She hadn't realised before, that love had its own light and perspective. Love. Love.

'Excuse me.'

Marian jumped. For a moment she could hardly think where she was.

The woman on the opposite side of the table, middle-aged, large-boned and gaunt, in a slippery-looking pale blue dress, was leaning towards her with an intimate smile. 'Excuse me.'

Had she been sighing or moaning to herself Marian wondered, feeling her cheeks for tears. 'Excuse me, but aren't you Elaine Bransome?'

'No. No. No.' Marian said on rising notes. 'No, I'm afraid you're quite mistaken.'

'Then you're her double. Weren't you at Manor Road School, Sutton Coldfield?'

Marian shook her head.

'Haven't you got any relations in Sutton Coldfield?'

Again she shook her head.

The woman's eyes, large and moist and battleship grey, seemed to be willing her to recall at least one distant relative. 'A cousin perhaps?' she persisted.

'Not as far as I know.'

Marian realised that the woman was determined to try to talk to her, and had a feeling that it was going to be both confessional and embarrassing, and she didn't even have a book to hide in.

She turned her eyes to the uninspiring urban countryside flashing by outside. Yellowish fields, straggly hedges, willows, a few thin riding-school ponies, a car dump. She watched as though engaged on a vitally important survey.

'She was a great friend of mine, Elaine Bransome was. Such a lovely girl. The only true friend I ever had. Very pretty too. You look so much like her.'

'Thank you,' Marian breathed at the window.

For a few minutes there was silence.

Then, 'I hope you don't think I've been rude,' the woman said. Marian had to turn towards her again. 'Of course not.'

'She was in the same class as me, only I had to leave when I was fifteen. That was when my mother died and I had to leave to look after my father and my little brothers and sisters. I didn't manage to finish my education.'

Marian said she was sorry.

The woman leaned further towards her. 'Are you educated?' she asked. 'Only you look educated. You look to me like a lady-doctor or one of these health visitors.'

Marian shook her head.

'Your husband looked very educated as well. And a gentleman.'

'Thank you,' Marian said. She relaxed back into her seat. For those words she was prepared to listen to the woman's life-story, sad and stormy as she knew it was going to be. Your husband.

'My husband was from the criminal classes. Of course I didn't know any better. You see I married at sixteen. Yes, to get away from my father. I expect you can guess what I mean? He couldn't leave me alone. Of course, I was sorry for him, him being a widower and me the image of my poor mum as he remembered her, but I couldn't put up with that, could I?'

Marian had tried to assume a suitable listening expression; interested, without being encouraging or prurient.

It didn't do for revelations of incest.

'Well, would you?' the woman asked, leaning so far over the table that she could feel her breath on her face.

'No,' Marian gulped. 'Oh no.'

'You might not think to look at me now, but I was a beauty, once, I was a beauty queen. Miss British Canals 1960. I was once a film extra. Escapade it was called. Did you happen to see it? What a pity. It was a wonderful film, not like the rubbish they have now. I saw it over and over again. This director kept putting me right in the front of every crowd scene. He said I should apply for a screen test. He said I was a natural. Only I never did. When you're married you don't, do you? If I had my time over again, I would. I'd do everything. The worst time was when he was in prison for the first time and I had two kids and had to have my auntie to live with me because I had this job working nights. Do you know what I missed most of all when he was in prison? A cup of tea in bed of a Sunday. You thought I was going to say something else, didn't you? No, he could be very considerate. "Have a lay-in," he used to say. "I'll have the babby." And he used to take her downstairs with him — I can still remember that lovely little snooze, perhaps it was only about five minutes before he brought me that cup of tea. It set me up for the day, that did. He wasn't a bad chap but he was never lucky. He was the one that was always caught. It lasted about twelve years, I suppose, though he was in prison about half the time. I never got married again after that. I could have, but I didn't bother. I had my kids, and a council flat and a nice little job. Well, men always drag you down, don't they, one way or another. I suppose your hubby isn't all he could be either? A bit of a lady's man, is he? A bit of a charmer?'

She leaned close, again.

'He's a perfect husband,' Marian said. 'We've been married twenty-three years and we've never had a cross word. We had three children; boy, girl, boy, but he was always considerate, doing his fair share of the house work and the shopping and the baby-minding. And now that they've all left home, we're like a pair of love-birds again.'

The woman stared at her blankly, then drew away, and after a few moments opened her magazine.

Marian sighed her relief, closed her eyes and fell asleep.

When she woke, perhaps an hour later, she found that a gently-nodding, elderly woman had joined the other on the opposite side of the table. 'My husband was from the criminal classes...I married him when I was sixteen...My father couldn't leave me alone...Miss British Canals...said I was a natural,' skimmed across the table to her.

Even from the safe distance of escape, Marian could feel the raw loneliness of the woman boring into her like a drill. The elderly woman was making sympathetic noises from time to time, and asking questions. Marian was ashamed that she had fobbed her off with lies, when all she'd wanted was a crumb of sisterly solidarity. I'm in the same boat, she wanted to cry out. We all are. Sally and I and even pretty Hannah. Why do we have such beautiful dreams, such ridiculous dreams? Where do they come from? Life is never easy, never what we want it to be.

She closed her eyes. The woman's droning voice wove itself into her sleep.

FIFTEEN

Marian's train arrived at the station only a few minutes late. She stood on the platform looking out for Sally or Gerald — she'd felt sure one or other of them would have come to save her having to get the bus — but there was no sign of either.

In spite of her sleep on the train, she felt tired and dispirited. It was cooler than the previous days, but not much. Her cotton dress was sticking to her hips, her feet ached. She decided to have a cup of tea in the Buffet before walking to the bus station.

The tea was purplish-grey and bitter. She stared at it morosely, wondering whether to leave it or try to summon up the energy to complain. If only there'd been some soft, dark, fruit cake to have with it, she thought. But it was a fact of life, or at least of her life, that in time of stress there was never any but plain yellow. Which tasted of talcum powder. She pushed away her tea cup.

'Mum.'

'Johnny. What are you doing here?'

Her elder son kissed her forehead and sat down next to her at the table. 'I've come to meet you,' he said. 'Gerald sent me.'

The sight of him brought the customary lump to her throat. She ran her hand down his arm, trying to make it seem a casual, almost accidental touching. 'How lovely to see you. When did you get home?'

'A couple of hours ago. Got a good hitch all the way from Salisbury.'

'Where's Tim? Is he with you?'

'No, but he'll soon be back. He won't be able to stay on. We had a terrific storm last night. All the tents were flooded.'

'How awful.'

'No, it was OK. This band went on playing and we went on drinking and messing about in the mud.'

She looked him over. To other eyes, he might seem moderately hale and hearty, to hers he was frail as a fledgling.

'I've had a bath now, as I hope you appreciate.'

'Yes, you look very clean.' (But surely paler than he should be?)

135

'I hope you don't mind me borrowing your trousers.'

'They're not mine. Is it likely I'd get into those? They must be Sally's. Yes, I think that's her shirt as well. Anyway, she won't mind. Isn't she back yet?'

'No.'

'Where can she be? Do you want a cup of tea?'

'No, I think we ought to get back. Gerald's in a state. In fact, in so much of a state that he forgot about not lending me his car.'

'Why didn't you bring mine?'

'Sally's taken it.'

'Well, I hope she hasn't had an accident. By the way, Virginia may be coming down for a few days. Gerald's having a party next Saturday.'

'Mum, let's go.'

Marian looked at John's profile as he was driving. He was so handsome, very like Dickie when she'd first met him. His hair was still very fair — it had once been silver-blond, almost white — and not so very much too long. All the same, she couldn't help noticing that he wasn't looking altogether happy.

'You look tense, darling,' she said, 'What's the trouble? Is Tim all right?' (Tell Mummy.)

'Tim's fine. It's just this business of Sally's. I can't say I understand all of it, but it's definitely worrying.' He sounded aggrieved.

John found all middle-aged people depressing. They were frivolous, flighty, preoccupied with sex; it was all that permissiveness forced on them in their formative years. The Sixties must have been hell to live through.

'Look, I know nothing about it,' Marian said. 'Couldn't I please be told something? I rang Gerald this morning and he said she hadn't got back since the storm. Has anything else happened?'

'Lots.'

'Watch the road, love.'

'Sorry about that. OK, where shall I start? You rang Gerald at ten this morning, right?'

'Right.'

'At about eleven, Gareth came over to see Paul. They'd had some sort of bust-up yesterday. I don't think we need bother much about that, except to establish that that was the reason he'd come over.

Gerald happened to be at Paul's when Gareth arrived. As far as I understand it, he'd gone to see if Paul could shed any light on Sally's disappearance. Why he should think Paul would have any information about her, I don't know, but again, that's besides the point.'

'She was looking after the shop yesterday, instead of me.'

'Oh, I see. Anyway, Paul makes everyone coffee. Gerald starts again on the case of the vanished lady. Gareth says; Sally, now was she a fortyish sort of woman in an F-registration metallic-blue Renault Five with grey upholstery? Gerald chokes a bit over that, but finally says yes and Gareth says he met her yesterday afternoon on Foel Graig; he'd actually taken shelter with her in the afore- mentioned car during the worst of the storm, even had some of her cheese sandwiches — quite good, he said they were — afterwards. That was at about five o'clock.'

'Whatever was she doing up there in a thunderstorm? And in my car? Honestly, Johnny, she's the limit.'

'Anyway, after the storm, Gareth drove off on his motor-bike.'

'And where did she go?'

'She was still there when he left.'

'Perhaps she couldn't get the car to start. Sometimes it won't. It's something to do with the automatic clutch. Automatic always means worse. He should have waited to see that she was all right.'

'That's exactly what Gerald said. He was, apparently, very annoyed with Gareth. And then Paul was very annoyed with Gerald. You can imagine.'

'Yes. But how did you get involved with it all?'

'The police insisted on questioning me.'

'The police? Do you mean Sgt. Howells?'

'No. Real policemen he'd got in from somewhere. Even though I'd only been back an hour, they seemed only too ready to consider me a possible abductor, rapist, murderer. Of course, that was before I'd had a bath and a shave.'

'I shouldn't have left home. I've been away less than thirty-six hours and I've come back to total chaos.'

'What did you do in London?'

'I can't remember. Go on about the police.'

'I think I'm going to leave the rest to Gerald. It starts to get complicated at that point. Oh, but listen, Mum. Before we arrive home, I ought to tell you something: I've brought this girl with me. And listen, she's important, right? Yeh, she's the one I told you about on the phone.'

'You never mentioned any girl.'

'I certainly meant to.'

'Thank you.'

'The thing is, we've been around together quite a while. Yeh, I'm pretty blissed-out about her. Try to be nice to her, Mum, will you? You know, don't *talk* to her or anything. No, of course I don't mean you're not to talk to her, but don't try to hold conversations with her, that's what I mean.'

'You mean, like we used to in the olden days?'

'Yeh. You know, just be natural. Don't make her feel she's a guest or something. And don't go on about where she's going to sleep or anything, because she'll be fine in Tim's room.'

'With Tim?'

'With both of us. I mean, she's been perfectly happy sharing our tent for the last three or four days.'

'She doesn't mind Tim's socks?'

'Oh, Mum, you always descend to such basics.'

'Sorry. I'll try to keep my few words crisp and clean. What's her name? If you say Mouse or Piglet I shall probably scream.'

'Stella.'

'Oh good. Stella. Is Tim bringing a girl as well?'

'Of course not...I mean, he's a kid, isn't he?'

Marian took a few deep breaths when John pulled up outside Gerald's house. She was so thankful that the weather had broken. She seemed to have enough to cope with, without all that blinding Continental sunshine as well.

'You've arrived back in one piece, then,' were Gerald's first words as she got out of the car, 'I'd forgotten what happened to the Mercedes when I asked John to meet you.'

'He drove perfectly. Yes, I've had a lovely time, thank you. I'm going in to have a cup of tea. Do you want to come with me and tell me about things?'

'I'm afraid the police want a word with you, Marian. They've got your car back. It's in Carmarthen being examined.'

'I'll see you later then, Mum.'

John loped away into the cottage, before Gerald could try to stop him. Why ever was her car being examined? For the first time,

Marian felt frightened about Sally. Gerald looked different, older, his face under the tan seemed grey and crêpey.

'Are they here now?' she asked him.

'Not at the moment. Come in and sit down and I'll fill you in with the details. What has John told you?'

She took a few more deep breaths. The hills in the distance looked blue and innocent. 'Sally's not back,' she said slowly, 'But there's no other cause for alarm, is there?'

'Come and sit down.'

Gerald led her into the drawing-room. White, pale-grey, a few touches of hyacinth blue and deep gold, Marian had always considered it a soothing room; Marjorie's. She sat in one of the deep arm-chairs and closed her eyes.

'Here you are,' Gerald said.

He handed her one of his very large whiskies.

Worse and worse, she thought as she accepted it. She didn't feel she could cope with a cup-of-tea problem, let alone a stiff-whisky one. She wondered if it would be insensitive to ask for a slice of cake. She took a quick look at Gerald and decided against it.

'Gareth is in trouble,' Gerald said quietly. 'Paul is almost out of his mind and worst of all Mrs Dainton's been in tears all afternoon, which has totally unnerved me.'

Marian took a large gulp of whisky. 'John got as far as Gareth meeting Sally on Foel Graig yesterday afternoon,' she said. 'Could you go on from there? Has anything else been heard of Sally?'

'Nothing whatsoever. She's disappeared, Marian. They're talking of getting a search party out. Perhaps they already have.'

'She's a very troublesome woman.'

'Have you eaten anything today?'

'Not much. A very stale pork pie and a packet of prawn-flavoured crisps.'

'I'll get you a beef sandwich. You always get aggressive when you're hungry. Now, don't drink on an empty stomach.'

Marian, heavy cut-glass tumbler in her hand, walked over to the window trying to fathom out where Sally could have got to. Why had she gone back to Foel Graig? She'd seemed very scornful of Gerald's enthusiasm for the place, when she'd returned from her trip with him on Thursday. Silly old Gerald, she'd called him more than once.

John was in the garden with a girl who must, she supposed, be

139

Stella. She waved and they waved back. Stella had waist-long dark hair, looked about seventeen, and... yes, very definitely pregnant.

She took another gulp of whisky.

'Here's your sandwich,' Gerald said. 'Sit down to eat it. Conserve your strength.'

'I drove up to the Graig,' Gerald said. 'And sure enough your car was there, exactly where Gareth had reported seeing it. But there was no sign of Sally anywhere. I walked about. I called her name. No sign of her. No reply. The silence seemed unusually eerie. It's the only time, I think, that I've ever felt uncomfortable up there. Well, after fifteen minutes or so, I drove back here and called on Sgt, Howells and when he heard all the details he immediately contacted a Detective Inspector Hudson from Head Office who was out here with a colleague in less than half an hour. And I'm afraid they've taken Gareth in for questioning.'

'Gareth? What madness. What can they think Gareth had to do with it?'

'That's what I thought. He seemed such a quiet, decent sort of chap.'

'He is a quiet, decent sort of chap.'

'Except that when I was out of the room, he confessed to Paul that he'd...that he'd...had sexual intercourse with her. With Sally. Can you believe it? What's the world coming to? And by this time he's probably confessed as much to the police as well.'

Marian was suddenly in fighting mood. 'Well, it may be surprising, Gerald, but it's not a crime, is it? I can understand Paul being upset about it, but I really can't see that it's a matter for the police.'

'But I suppose they'd have to take the possibility of sexual assault into account — rape. After all, he admitted that he'd never met her before. Could she have been a willing party? With this youth she just happened to run into?'

'When are the police coming to question me?' Marian asked, standing up again and walking towards the window.

'Oh God, Paul's coming up the drive,' Gerald said. 'He's in a bad way. Can you cope with him?'

'Of course I can cope with him. But Gerald, would you mind leaving us on our own, please?'

Everyone seemed changed. Paul was red-eyed and dishevelled, his shirt and trousers looking as though they'd been slept in.

He walked into the room with exaggerated weariness. 'What a balls-up,' he said. He came up to Marian and kissed her.

'Paul, love,' she said, hugging him back.

'Oh Marian, I'm sorry to involve you in my wretched affairs.'

'I've wanted to be involved. You know that. I've asked and asked. Now, tell me everything. Please.' She hugged him again. Paul lay back in one of the pale armchairs, his long legs stretched out in front of him.

'You see, Gareth was going to leave his wife,' he said, 'but when it came to it, it turned out to be much more difficult than he'd thought.'

He sighed, sat up, looked Marian straight in the eyes, sighed again. 'I went over there yesterday morning to lend him some support, but his wife, Susan, was terribly cut-up and bitter. The thing is, he hadn't really thought she'd be so upset. Neither had I. Well, I'd hardly thought of her at all. Anyway, the result was that he went off on his motor-bike to this Graig place to think things over.'

'He must have been in a pretty bad state.'

'That's right.'

'In that sort of state when you'll turn to anyone for any crumb of comfort they can offer you.'

'Exactly. And this woman turns up... Sally, I mean. And she was so friendly towards him. And he was able to confide in her because she was a total stranger. Can you understand that?'

'Absolutely.'

Paul stopped talking. She saw him struggling to understand the thing that had happened next. He got to his feet, walked to the marble fireplace and seemed to be examining it carefully. He picked up a blue and white vase from the mantlepiece and turned his attention to that.

'And now they think he raped her, for God's sake,' he said, returning the vase to its place and coming back to sit down.

'What nonsense,' Marian said. '*She* seduced *him*. I know her. I'll tell them what happened. They'll believe me. She's my friend, my best friend. What motive would I have for lying?'

'Could you really tell them that?'

'Of course. It's the truth. I must tell them.'

A discreet cough from the hall told her that Gerald was about to come in with an offer of tea or more whisky. 'But we must find Sally,' she said. 'The police will be on the wrong track. They'll be looking in the sort of places where one would dispose of a body, that's what they're trained for. But Sally's alive, I'm certain of that, so we must look in quite different places.'

Gerald came in.

'We must go at once,' she told him. 'We need you to show us where the car was. I'll find her. I'll know exactly where to look for her.'

'Will your mother be all right on her own?' she asked Paul.

'Miss Morris is with her.'

'So that's fine. Let's go quickly Gerald, before anything else happens.'

'Are you sure...?' Gerald started to ask.

'Yes, I'm sure.'

SIXTEEN

Do you want to come with us? To look for Sally?' Marian called to John and his girlfriend who were sitting in the garden with the Sunday papers.

'Do you mind if we don't,' John said. 'We've done a hell of a lot of walking today.'

He came over to the car, pulling Stella by the hand. 'Mum, this is Stella,' he said.

'Hello Stella. You've met Gerald, haven't you? And Paul? I hope John's given you something to eat. Perhaps you could make us one of your curries later on, John? Anyway, we must be off. See you later.'

'Wasn't that rather off-hand, Marian?' Gerald asked her, after he'd started the car and pulled away. 'She seems a nice little thing. I can't see why you should snub her.'

'Good Lord, Gerald, you *are* out of touch. They think you're patronising them if you make small-talk. I'm always being told off about it.'

'Are they thinking of getting married?'

'I shouldn't think so. Why? John's got another year at college.'

'Is she at college?'

'I know nothing about her Gerald. Nothing.'

'Anyway, you musn't worry, Marian. John is a very capable young man. He'll make his way in the world sooner or later. And perhaps having a wife... a girl-friend... and... some responsibilities will steady him.'

'It may seem dreadful, Gerald, but I can't give them much thought at the moment. I've suddenly got too much on my mind. I feel...'

'Gerald,' Paul suddenly said from the back of the car. 'I don't think I should come with you. Gareth may phone. Or he may come back, later on. I feel I should be at home.'

Gerald stopped the car. 'Just as you like, old fellow,' he said in a subdued voice. 'Shall I run you back?'

'No, I'll walk from here. A walk will do me good.'

As he got out of the car, he patted Marian's shoulder. 'Sorry,' he said.

She smiled at him. Then, as the car drove on, turned and waved with as much cheer as she could muster.

'Poor old Paul,' Gerald said. 'That Gareth seems a pretty unsavoury specimen. There's something very unstable about homosexuals, say what you like.'

'There's something very unstable about people,' Marian said glumly. 'Say what you like about that.'

She was beginning to feel more and more tired and bewildered. The pace of her life, set at slow and steady for so long, now seemed to be switched to fast and furious. When all she wanted was a few quiet moments to re-live that brief time — only half a day and a night — with Alan; a few moments to count the measure of her wealth. Would she ever see him again? She was afraid the episode would fade into a dream. It already seemed unreal. Alan, she said to herself, summoning him. Again she rang the bell of the little basement flat in Finsbury. Alan.

'I could write a poem about your feet,' John said. 'They're almost my favourite part. Your heels, so round and rosy. Such elegant little toes. This little greyhound went to market. This little greyhound stayed at home. Will you go to sleep if I go on stroking them like this?'

' "Place the pork between two sheets of greaseproof paper or cling-film,"' Stella read out from one of the Sunday supplements. '"Beat out thinly with a rolling pin. Finely chop the mushrooms. Peel, core and chop the apple. Sauté the apple and mushrooms in the oil for a few minutes until the apple begins to soften." Mmm, doesn't it sound wonderful? "Dry cider, whole grain mustard, fresh brown bread-crumbs, chopped parsley. Serve immediately with a crisp green salad." No thanks. I'd rather it with roast potatoes, fresh peas and buttered parsnips. What do you think?'

'Stella's feet are my delight
Bone and sinew, arch and curve,' John intoned.

'"Paprika-grilled poussin," Hm. Sounds a bit pretentious. "Beat together .... pre-heat the grill .... spoon on the remaining mixture and cook for a further four or five minutes or until juices run clear when the flesh is pierced with a skewer." Yum, yum, yum. "Serve with a hot salad of courgettes and toasted pine kernels garnished with slices of lemon."'

She pulled away from him. 'My feet will drop off if I don't have a meal soon,' she said crossly. 'You said your mother would have a Sunday roast.'

She tucked her feet up under her wide, pink skirt.

'I didn't know she was going to London for the weekend,' John said. 'Be fair.'

'There must be some food in the house. I'm your guest. Make me a meal.'

'Let's go to bed,' he said.

'No.' She picked up the magazine again.

'My parents always went to bed on a Sunday afternoon. Tim and I used to wonder why they were thumping about, it seemed so different from their usual quiet behaviour. They used to say they were doing the crossword puzzle.'

'"Serve immediately with crusty rolls and creamed leeks,"' she read out as she saw the way he was looking at her. 'Do you like leeks?'

'Not much! Hey! I can't see why you should knock me about because of that.'

'How can we ever be happy together if you don't like leeks?'

'I could probably get to like them. I'll try. They smell nice, but I don't like the texture much. Aren't they a tiny bit slimy?'

'Of course they're not slimy.'

Stella turned. She sat on the grass, close to his deck-chair, pressing up against his legs. Her back was straight and flat. The backs of her arms were paler than any other part of her body, a shiny creamy colour like toadstools and her elbows were round and smooth, almost as beautiful as her little pink heels. Previously he'd only noticed breasts and legs. But when one was in love there was so much more. He wondered if he dared mention her elbows. She'd become sensitive about her body. Some days she'd hardly let him as much as glance at her lovely belly, curving upwards like a magnolia flower. Belly was an ugly word; he'd searched through the *Oxford Book of Verse* for a nice quotation, but all he'd come up with was, 'Thy belly is like an heap of wheat,' from the Song of Solomon. Perhaps it sounded better in Hebrew.

He laid a tentative hand on her belly.

To his surprise, Stella put her hand over his and crumpled up against him. 'It's awful, isn't it,' she said — she was usually so brave — 'Why did this have to happen to us?'

John could feel a fine sweat breaking out on his back as he tried to think of the right thing, or even *any* thing, to say.

145

'No, I can't see that it's too awful,' he said at last. 'Think of all the people who spend ten years — and all their savings — trying to have a baby.'

'It must be quite rare to have one when you have a thingummy fitted — as well as all that horrible jelly. Oh God, we're going to be so poor. You said your mother would help us, but I don't think she will. I don't think she took to me.'

'Of course she did. Of course she took to you. She was pre-occupied, that's all. Surely you can understand that? Anyway, we'll get by, even if she doesn't help us. It's only for a year.'

'If Tim leaves us we'll be done for. We'll have to move from the flat to something even smaller and more squalid.'

'Tim is not going to leave us and there isn't anything more squalid.'

'He said he was going to the South of France with that Norwegian girl.'

'He won't. It's just talk. He won't even go to the dentist without me.'

They both thought of Tim still at the Festival. Free as air.

'I can't be a mother, though, John. I'm not sensible enough to look after a baby. I'll lose him. Like I lose my purse and my keys and my library books. I'll put him in a carrier bag and leave him on a bus. No, I'm serious. I don't feel I can take it on.'

John forbore to mention how she had steadfastly refused even to discuss an abortion. She took life as it came, she'd said. Whatever was chucked at her.

'OK. Then I'll leave college as well, and we'll take it on between us,' he said. 'I've always been careful and sensible. I never lose things.'

'You make it sound easy, but it won't be.'

They were both terrified.

'It won't be easy, but it might be quite fun,' John said.

'We're too young to settle down.'

'Plenty of people have babies when they're sixteen. We're nearly twenty-one. Knocking on a bit, really. Anyway, we don't have to settle down. People take babies with them everywhere. Across de-serts and oceans. Everywhere.'

'We're not taking our baby everywhere,' Stella said.

'OK, I agree with you. But we don't have to settle down in a semi-detached suburban house with a neat little lawn back and front. That's all I meant.'

They each rejected such a house, though not without a struggle.

'I suppose we'll get fond of him,' Stella said after a long silence.

'Of course we will. I'm fond of him already. Lying there in the snug of that beautiful belly.'

'I suppose we'll take him to the swings in the park and the laundrette.'

'Will we take him camping next summer?'

'Not to the Festival. The babies there all looked a bit shell-shocked, I thought.'

'We could always bring him here and leave him with Mum. She likes babies. She's always peering into prams.'

'Only she'll give him sweets and chocolates.'

'Oh, she'll certainly spoil him. We'll have to accept that. She was pretty lax with us. Tim could always get away with anything.'

'She looks quite nice. At least she looks motherly. Different from my mother. I don't know how I'm going to tell her. She'll be absolutely furious. Her generation are all on the pill and think they're so clever.'

'You won't have to tell her anything, love. Just arrange to meet her. Invite her to Gerald's party. Ring her up. Gerald won't mind, specially not if you ask him. He was freaked out by you. I thought he was never going to let go your hand. I wonder if he's a dirty old man?'

'I shouldn't think so. Not more than most old men.'

'Last summer, Tim and I thought Mum was going to marry him. He was always over here, washing-up and so on. But they must have decided against it.'

'Pity in a way. He's got a wonderful house for grandchildren.'

'No, it's much too smart. He's obsessive about his carpets.'

He thought of the time he and Tim had hidden an almost full bottle of very good Burgundy under the sofa to take home with them. Only to find that some idiot had kicked it over; the cork they'd so carefully pushed in had managed to get dislodged and the wine had seeped out on to the carpet which had had to be professionally cleaned. And though there were over fifty people at the party, Gerald had taken it for granted that he and Tim were responsible, which was a bit thick. He'd suggested to his mother that she should pay for the professional cleaning, since Gerald never tired of bringing it up, but she'd been very huffy about it. He shouldn't give parties, she'd said, if he couldn't afford to clean up after them. (She'd gone on to tell them about a birthday party they'd once had, when a child called Tamsin Isaacs had been sick five times on the way from the dining room to the downstairs cloakroom. And that had been on hair-cord. John could remember Tamsin quite well. She had a nice little round face and a marvellous go-cart. She'd sat next to Tim in school one week, when her friend Nicola Fairclough had had whooping-cough and she'd let him suck her thumb. Girls were always being sweet to Tim.)

Stella was looking happy again. When she's happy, I'm happy, he thought. That certainly seemed like love.

'This is where Gareth brought us this morning,' Gerald said, drawing up on to a grassy plateau where the single-track road petered out.

Marian got out of the car, and to her surprise, felt immediately invigorated. The mountains were beautiful, wild and ancient and free. Drifts of heather, mauve and pink, on the dark grey shale, long blue shadows, blue distances. A huge sky, flocked with pearly clouds. A whipping wind. Everything fresh and new-rinsed.

She could imagine — feel — how excited Sally would be in this breathtaking setting, a queen coming in to her domain. And her success with the young man, Gareth, burning in her brain and her body. What would she do? Gareth, probably feeling chastened and ashamed, would have ridden off on his motor-bike; she would hardly have noticed his going. The storm would have left the air charged with electricity.

What would she do? She'd climb right up to the top of the mountain, that's what she'd do. And in the most unsuitable shoes if Marian knew anything about it.

'We're wasting our time up here,' Gerald said, shouting against the wind. 'The police may have had a search-party out by this time. All the same, we may as well go as far as the stone again. Gareth said they'd walked as far as that.'

'You go that way,' Marian said. 'I'm going up to the top.'

'That's further away than it seems, Marian. It's still quite a way from here. Sally wouldn't have gone scrambling up there with the thunder still rumbling all around her.'

'Yes she would,' Marian said.

SEVENTEEN

Miss Morris liked to go to chapel on a Sunday evening, but decided she should forgo it for once in order to stay with Mrs Dainton.

She suggested that they should listen to the hymns on television.

Hymns, Mrs Dainton thought. Still, I suppose I'd better get used to them. I bet they'll have all these sorts of programmes in the Rest Home, though why they think the elderly want to waste their time listening to hymns beats me — I'd rather have sex and violence any day. And at Christmas, they'll have all the children's choirs coming in and singing carols and playing recorders. Or perhaps it'll be harps in this part of the world, which is even worse. And His Worship the Mayor will have his picture took with the eldest resident — I can't wait, I don't think — and then a few more carols, and then the smallest children will act a Nativity play. Nativity plays. Seen one, seen them all, it seems to me. And this is the way the world ends, with hymns and carols and Nativity plays. Still, the residents would probably rather have anything happening than nothing. It's a bit like being in prison, I suppose, though perhaps the sentences are shorter.

'This is one of my favourites,' Miss Morris said. 'Do you mind if I turn it up a bit?'

Miss Morris thought of those evenings when she'd gone to chapel with her sweetheart Glyn Parry from Llanddu. She'd got a pale grey tailor-made costume that summer, and a blouse in a colour they called eau-de-nil. White gloves if she remembered rightly. They'd shared a hymn-book, but had both been too shy to sing and only longed for the service to be over so that they could walk back across Park Meadow to his auntie's house where he left his bicycle. (His auntie would be watching them from behind her lace curtains, but she never waved or showed that she'd seen them. She was a strange little woman who washed dishes in the Red Lion. People said she liked a drink herself.)

Her life would have been altogether different if Glyn Parry had come back from the war. She'd be a grandmother by now perhaps, perhaps several times over. She could still remember his eyes, a very

149

pale blue like faded speedwell, with something very sweet and sad in the shape of them. She was pleased to remember how she'd stood up to her mother over the matter of the engagement ring. This was my choice she said, I don't care for solitaires. Well, she'd got them both now, Glyn's little ring and her mother's big diamond, and nobody to leave them to. Eau-de-nil was a foolish name for a colour that was only a sort of green.

He is one among ten thousand,
And above all earthly joys,
Let me linger in his presence night and day.

She sang the last hymn with the congregation, her pretty voice cracking a little, her not-quite-plain face uplifted.

'You see, he left me a nice legacy as well as the house I was living in,' Mrs Dainton said when Miss Morris had quite finished the fancy Amen. 'It gives me a bit of independence, doesn't it?'

'Your husband?' Miss Morris asked.

'Well, by that time, he was someone else's husband, the dirty rat. All the same, he didn't forget me, not even in his will. He left nothing to wifey. She was rich, I grant you, but she must have felt it. Not that I shed any tears for her. Well, after a few years I sold the house and bought this shop for Paul, and I think he's making it pay at last, which means I can spend the money I've got left on the fees for Greystones, which is the best Old People's Home in the area, according to Dr Ansell.'

Miss Morris sighed. She'd spent the greater part of the afternoon trying to dissuade Mrs Dainton from a hasty and unconsidered decision regarding a Home, but she might as well have saved her breath.

'You could always give it a try, I suppose,' she said. 'Come back here if it doesn't suit you. Though I'm sure Paul will be very lonely. I wish he'd come out of his room for a bit of a chat. I wonder if he'd like me to make him a little snack? Bacon and eggs perhaps, or cheese on toast?'

'Why don't you go and ask him? He had next to nothing for his lunch.'

I never had many good points, but I was never greedy for money, I'll say that, Mrs Dainton told herself, when she'd sent Miss Morris away to bother Paul. He was unemployed when I married him and poor as a parson. The first house we rented didn't even have running water — except down the wall. A real dump. I can remember the smell of that back-kitchen even now; flood water and soot with a suspicion of cat pee. The wallpaper in the bedroom was pink roses round a trellis-work and there was so much mould growing on it, you could really think the garden had come inside. But I didn't complain. Well, I probably did complain, knowing me, but I didn't really mind it. We had a good time in that house, in spite of everything. When he got a job and we moved to a better place, I was pregnant and the best was over. After the war, he did start making money, but he'd got mean about spending it by that time. He was after status, then, all those things like a big car and golf clubs and clean shirts. When he met *her*, half her attraction was that her father was a managing director of something-or-other and that their house had two bathrooms and a swimming pool in the garden. When he told me he was going to marry her, I was sick and furious, yes, but I didn't care a penny whistle for the money I'd be losing, though I pretended it was all I minded. The only money I've ever really cared for is what he left me in his will. Because that was a sign he still thought of me and loved me. More than he loved old Fat Arse anyway. What became of her, I wonder. Not that I care.

'He won't have anything, Mrs Dainton. He's going out again. But he's promised me that he'll make himself a proper meal as soon as he knows Gareth's in the clear. I have a feeling he may be going over to their house, to see if his wife knows anything. That's only a guess, mind.'

Miss Morris was about to sit again, when she heard a tap at the door. 'Visitors,' she told Mrs Dainton, plumping up the cushions and pushing the *News of the World* under a chair.

'Some young people to see you,' she said then, bringing in John and Stella.

John had thought that having Stella to look at and wonder about and question, might raise Mrs Dainton's spirits, but she hardly seemed to notice her.

'I've come to tell you that you're not to worry any more about Paul's friend,' he said. 'Mum's certain she'll be able to get everything sorted out. She told me to tell you that Sally's always doing stupid things and causing trouble.'

'We know Gareth wouldn't hurt a fly,' Miss Morris said in her nice, quiet voice. 'We're not at all worried about that aspect of the matter, are we Mrs Dainton? We're upset for Paul's sake, that's all.'

'In what way, Miss Morris?' John asked.

Miss Morris didn't answer, only looked hard at him, suggesting perhaps, that he should ask no more questions.

Mrs Dainton spoke for the first time. 'I didn't know Gareth was married,' she said. 'That took me aback, that did.'

'I didn't think you'd let anything bother you,' John said in a bantering tone. 'I thought you prided yourself on being broad-minded. You told me once that you believed in freedom, in everyone being free as air.'

'So I do.'

'So there you are. Gareth's marriage is in his way and he wants out,'

'No,' Miss Morris said gently. 'No, he told Paul this morning that he was going back to his wife. They both think they can start again and make a go of it. His wife seems a sensible young woman. She told Gareth that they were equally to blame. She admitted she'd always been too wrapped up in the children. They're going to try and make a new start.'

'I see,' John said quietly. 'So that's why Paul's looking so sick.'

'And now Mrs Dainton has somehow got it into her head that the best thing for her to do is to move to this Rest Home at Amroth as soon as possible. I'm trying to persuade her that Paul will need her company more than ever at the moment. Don't you think so, now, John?'

'I certainly wouldn't do anything in a hurry,' John said. 'I can't see that you'd be helping anyone by moving out now.'

'It's not in a hurry. It's been on my mind for quite a time. I'm getting that I can't dress myself. I can afford to be looked after properly, so why not?'

Stella had been looking around her with great interest. She loved Thirties furniture and bric à brac. She'd only paid attention to the last part of the conversation.

'Perhaps you're right, ' John said uncertainly.

'I think it's a very stupid idea,' Stella said.

They all turned to look at her as though they'd almost forgotten she was there.

'I think you'd be mad to leave here — where you've got your independence — just because of some boring trouble with your son. If you've got money, use it. Why should other people get the benefit of it? How could you leave this lovely room, all this lovely furniture, all your nice things? How could you? Could you bear to live in one of these big smart places with horrible matching sofas and somebody else's pictures on the wall, and people calling you 'we'?'

'You're not the sort to sit around quietly in an Old People's Home,' John said, taking courage from Stella. 'You wouldn't like the other old people for a start, they'd all be old. You can't stand old people. You always say you can't stand the vicar and he's only about fifty.'

'You could pay some young person to come to look after you, to do your hair and so on. Or just to sit and talk to you if that's what you want. Somebody unemployed would be very pleased to have a job like that. I know I would, if I lived around here,' Stella said.

'It would mean you wouldn't get on Paul's nerves and he wouldn't get on yours,' John added. 'It would mean he could go out without feeling guilty because you'd have someone else for at least part of every day.'

'It's not such a bad idea,' Miss Morris said. 'And as a matter of fact there's a young woman who lives in the flat across the road, she was asking Miss Morris-Jones at the library if she knew anyone who wanted a daily help. She's been unemployed for six months, she said. She looks a bit on the rough side, mind, but looks aren't every- thing.'

'We could make some enquiries tomorrow,' Stella said. 'John and I. Why don't we ask her to come to see you?'

'Only I don't know whether she'd suit Paul,' Miss Morris said in a small voice.

'We're not intending her for Paul,' Mrs Dainton said sharply. 'He's not that way inclined.'

She thought of the bold-faced young woman from the flat across the road, of the discussions and arguments they'd have. She would- n't do a hand's turn of work, she was sure of that, but she might have some tales to tell. She suddenly felt wonderfully recovered — John's girl-friend was a sharp one, and no mistake.

Stella had settled back in her chair again, looking as though she'd never spoken. 'Will you have a nice cup of tea?' Miss Morris asked her. 'I brought over some light-cakes — I did some baking this morning — will you try some? Or would you prefer some speckled bread? With butter and this year's strawberry jam?'

'She'd like some of everything, please,' John said.

'It was good to see them eat, wasn't it?' Miss Morris said after they'd gone. 'She was a pretty little thing, I thought, and very sensible. I wonder what Mrs Reed thinks of it all? Well, there's not the same disgrace now, is there? It's a different world, and better too, in many ways. I remember a girl called Gwenda Rees becoming pregnant during the war — one of these smart American boys, so people said — and she couldn't stand the disgrace, poor thing. Do you know what she did? She took a train all the way to Bournemouth and drowned herself there. Would you credit it now? And us with coasts all around us, so what was the call to go all that distance? I expect she wanted people to think she was going off to marry somebody. She hoped, I daresay, her body wouldn't be found and identified, and it wasn't for a month or so. Poor Mrs Rees, she was never the same afterwards. Mr Rees, a postman he was before the war, was killed in North Africa, and that baby could have been such a comfort to his widow, but no-one would have dared say so in those days.'

Mrs Dainton stared coldly in front of her saying nothing. On a day of such momentous happenings and decisions, she didn't see why her affairs should be elbowed aside for a fifty-year-old tragedy, however poignant.

'It's a different world,' Miss Morris said again, trying not to think of poor Gwenda Rees on that train. Trying not to think of the past. The present was better, in many ways.

EIGHTEEN

At first, Marian thought Sally was dead. She'd come across her by accident, stumbling into the hollow where she was lying.

When she found she was still breathing, she tried to rouse her; calling her name and slapping her face.

'Sally. Sally. Come on Sally, wake up.' It was like the old days when they were at University. Sally, you're late. You must get up. You'll miss your bus.

Sally opened her eyes. 'Marian,' she said. She tried to move towards her, but slumped back, groaning with pain.

'I'll have to get help,' Marian said. Had Sally broken her leg, she wondered. She wouldn't contemplate anything worse. 'Gerald is not far away. He'll fetch an ambulance.'

'Don't leave me,' Sally said, suddenly gripping her with surprising strength. 'I've been so frightened. I'm going out of my mind. I've had such dreadful nightmares. I've been here for days.'

'It must seem like days. It's actually only twenty-four hours. But that's long enough, God knows. Too long. You must let me go. You need a doctor. You desperately need something to drink. No wonder you've been hallucinating.'

'Oh, I've had such dreams, Marian. Do you suppose this is a tomb?'

'No, I shouldn't think so. They're at the top of the mountain, aren't they.'

'I've been so cold and frightened.'

She seemed calmer. Marian made another effort to get away from her.

'Gerald is not far away.' She tried to speak calmly. 'He'll know what to do. I'll come straight back and stay with you while he drives to the nearest phone to get help. They'll be able to bring an ambulance most of the way. They'll have you in hospital in no time, I promise you. You must be brave for another five minutes.'

This time, Marian thought she was going to be able to get away, but at the last moment, Sally lunged at her and clung to her again. 'I won't let you go. I won't. I'd rather die than stay here again by myself. If Gerald is here, shout to him. He'll find us. He'll come to find us.

Shout to him.'

'Help,' Marian shouted. 'Help. Help. Help.' She could feel the wind tearing her voice from her throat and buffeting it away. 'Gerald,' she shouted. 'Gerald.'

'He won't be able to hear me,' she whispered. 'You must let me stand up so that I can shout properly.'

But Sally was afraid she'd break away from her. She clung on to her with what seemed like superhuman strength.

After a few minutes, Marian lay down by her side to comfort her. I'll have to wait till she loses consciousness again, she thought. Even in the poor light she could see the pain in Sally's face.

'I'm so cold,' Sally said, shivering and trembling. 'Oh Marian, this is such a terrible place. I got what I came for, and then had to pay for it, had to stay imprisoned in this place waiting for death.'

'You're not going to die, Sally.'

'All my life, I've been so selfish, so self-obsessed.'

'At least you've never been boring,' Marian said impatiently, 'and I hope you're not going to start now. I couldn't bear it if you're going to start moaning and begging people to forgive you and all that rubbish.'

'It's not rubbish. I want people to forgive me. Especially you, Marian. Will you? Please?' She squeezed her hand.

'Of course I will. Haven't I always done whatever you've asked me to?' She was trying not to cry.

'You're not taking me seriously. I've never been so serious in my life. I've been lying here re-living my past.'

Like Richard the Third and Scrooge, Marian thought, and The Man Who Fell Among Thieves. 'Poor Sally,' she said. 'Buck up now, though, or you'll have this little scene to regret as well.'

'All the things I've never bothered to do. I've never helped people, never visited people in hospital. I've never really noticed nature. I've never gone to concerts. I've travelled, but I've never really taken the trouble to see things. When we went to Greece, all I did was lie about in the sun. If Alan and Virginia went to Delphi and all those other places, I thought it let me out. I've never lived life fully.'

In that case, I've never lived at all, Marian thought.

'And Virginia. I've never given her half enough attention.'

'The boys used to think she was so lucky. That's what all youngsters want, Sally, mothers who leave them alone. Come on, it's not like you to be so wet. Get a hold of yourself.'

156

'Help,' Marian shouted. 'Gerald. Gerald. We're here. Here. Here. Here.'

Her shouting alarmed a company of rooks which began to circle about, cawing raucously for a few moments.

'Shout again,' Sally said, 'He'll hear the birds and realise that something's disturbed them.'

Marian repeated her shouts, over and over again, again and again, until she fell back exhausted. Where can he have got to? she wondered. Why doesn't he come?

Now Sally's whole weight seemed to be on her and Marian realised that she must have fainted again. She tried to worm herself free, shuffling inch by inch from under her. After a very long slow struggle, and when she'd almost managed to get away, Sally came to again and gripped her as tightly as before.

'I've got cramp,' Marian said. 'You must let me get up. You must let me go and get help.'

'Help?' Sally said. 'There's no-one here. Why did we come here? I can't remember.'

Her voice had changed.

'You came here straight from the shop. You were looking after the shop while I went to London.'

'I can't remember,' Sally said again. 'I can't remember the shop,'

Marian felt alarmed at her voice. 'Of course you remember. You wanted me to go to see Alan. Of course you remember.' She wanted to shake her.

The wind was rising. The rooks had started to call again. It seemed to be getting darker by the minute.

Marian was almost in despair. What could she do? Why didn't Gerald come?

Sally drew her head away and started to speak again. 'This is holy ground,' she said in a frightened voice. 'You know that, don't you? This is the land of the Goddess. She kept me here to punish me. You know that don't you? Every night she came to me. She was angry with me.'

'Stop it, stop it,' Marian said. 'You're frightening yourself and me. Stop it. Can't you see that you've imagined it all? You've been here all alone. You've been alone and in pain. That's all. That's all.'

'I've been alone and in pain,' Sally said, like a child repeating a lesson.

'You've been thirsty, too, very thirsty. You've had nightmares. It's not surprising.'

There was silence all around them. Marian began to wonder if they might have to face another night on the mountain.

'And when it was light, the birds came,' Sally said, in the same high voice. 'You know that, don't you? Everyone knows about the birds, the birds of Rhiannon.'

'Yes,' Marian said, deciding that it might be better to humour her. 'I know about the birds. I've read about them. Gerald's told me about them. Adar Rhiannon. They sing to comfort us, to let us sleep and forget our pain.'

She stroked Sally's head as she crooned the words that seemed to come out of her subconscious mind. She found herself swaying her body to the tune of the chanting words.

She lost all sense of time.

When was it that Sally stirred and next spoke? Was it five minutes or an hour later?

'Oh Marian, I remember now. A young man — a young boy — brought me up here on the back of his motor bike. What was his name? I shouldn't have let him bring me up here.'

Marian was so relieved at the change in her that she could hardly speak. 'Gareth. His name was Gareth.'

'Yes. He was a sweet, gentle boy. But why did he leave me here? Were you with us?'

'I'd gone to London, Sally. Do you remember taking me to catch the train?'

There was another long silence.

'Yes, I remember that. But I can't remember much more. My head aches when I try to remember coming up here. Why did I come?'

'Don't try to remember. You may have knocked your head when you fell. But listen; this is important. That young boy you were with — Gareth — is in trouble with the police. Do you understand? They think he raped you. They've taken him away to question him. Think how awful it is for him. I must let them know you're here safe and sound. You're going to let me go aren't you? Because Gareth — that nice young boy — is in trouble.'

Sally didn't answer but Marian could feel her arms slackening their hold. Something had got through to her.

After a moment or two, Marian managed to roll her over on to her side. She thought she might have lost consciousness again, but her eyes were open wide and looking at her.

'Will you be long?' she asked, her voice child-like and frightened.

'No. I'll be very, very quick. I'll put my jacket over you. Everything's going to be all right. Don't think of anything but that. You're safe.'

She bent to stroke her face, not daring to go too near in case she suddenly grabbed at her again. 'You're safe,' she repeated.

She started to scramble down towards the car. I mustn't fall, she kept telling herself. Everything's going to be all right as long as I don't fall.

She reached the car and saw that Gerald was sitting in it, slumped over the wheel.

Wherever have you been, she wanted to ask. I called and called. I thought you'd follow me when I didn't come back.

'What is it, Gerald?' she asked gently.

'Some sort of a turn, Marian. Almost blacked-out. Managed to drag myself back here. Ashamed of myself. Nothing like this ever happened to me before.'

Marian slackened his tie and opened the other doors of the car. 'You'll soon be all right,' she said, 'Don't worry. You've been under a lot of strain.'

His hands were very cold. She blew on them and chafed them.

'You look better already,' she said. 'You'll soon be yourself again.'

'No trace of Sally?' he said, after a moment or two.

'Yes. But she's broken her leg or something. She's in quite a bad way. She's in a sort of shallow trench near the top.'

'I know the place.' (He didn't tell her what it was.) 'Thank God you found her. We must go to the garage just beyond the first cross-roads to phone for an ambulance.'

Gerald was in the driving seat. It took several minutes to get him to the passenger seat. His face looked deathly pale again after the effort of trying to move.

'You haven't got a tablet you can take?' Marian asked him.

'Nothing. I've never had a turn like this before.'

She mopped his forehead with the handkerchief she found in the pocket of his jacket. 'Where are your keys?' she asked him.

'In my trouser-pocket. I can't seem to reach them.'

'Don't worry. Don't worry about anything.'

She managed to get the keys and to start the car.

159

It was a very difficult turn; the grass wet and muddy. She'd always refused to drive Gerald's large car, even on proper roads. I mustn't panic, she kept telling herself, trying not to think of Sally's face as she'd left her. Everything's going to be fine.

'Are you OK, Gerald?'

'Yes. You're doing very well. Slowly does it. Very slowly here.'

What if the garage is closed, she thought. What time is it? Where will I find a phone box? Will I ever reach the road? Poor Gerald looks ghastly. I'm so worried about Sally. Please God, don't let me panic. It's going to be all right. Everything 's going to be all right.

At the foot of the mountain, where the track joined the minor road she could see a police-car which seemed to be about to drive away. She hooted at them.

'A police-car, Gerald,' she said. 'God, they're not going to stop,'

She pressed the horn, over and over again. The car slowed down and waited. As she drew up behind it, two policemen came towards them.

'You were told to wait for us, Sir,' one of them said when he saw Gerald. 'We've failed to find the place where the car was. These bloody hills all look alike.'

'We need an ambulance,' Marian said, bursting into tears.

NINETEEN

Gerald was allowed home from the hospital the next afternoon. After several tests, it had been concluded that he had not, after all, had a heart attack.

Marian, who had seen him collapsed over the wheel of his car, his face waxen, was sceptical of the result.

'I'm delighted you're home,' she said, 'but all the same, I'm not so sure they should have let you come. Anyway, you must take whatever it was as a warning, and slow down a bit. Have you got a friend who could come to stay with you for a week or two? I'm sure you ought to have a complete rest. Is there anyone you could...?'

'I shall go on as usual,' he said stiffly. 'I've weathered much worse than this. Now, stop being officious and tell me about Sally. Have you seen her?'

'Not since last night, but I've just heard that she's out of Intensive Care. Her leg is broken in two places, but at least her mind seems back to normal. Why did she go up there, that's what I can't understand.'

'Didn't you ask her?'

'She couldn't remember. She must have had a terrible night there, all alone in that storm. No wonder she was raving: Voices. Voices in the night. The birds of Rhiannon — I suppose she heard the dawn chorus. Is there a dawn chorus on a mountain?'

'The birds of Rhiannon,' Gerald said slowly and importantly, as Marian knew he would. 'Yes, I was telling her about them the other day. They're probably as old as the oldest myth in the world. No-one knows exactly why they sang or to whom, but they're always assumed to have been a source of comfort. They sang to Branwen and the seven warriors when they returned from Ireland to the Island of the Mighty. "Alas son of God, said she, woe is me that ever I was born. Two good islands have been laid waste because of me".'

'I can't say I experienced much comfort up there,' Marian cut in. 'I was frightened out of my mind. How long was I there? I still don't

161

know. Did you ever feel, when you were there, that time had stopped? That you were somehow outside time?'

Gerald didn't seem to be going to answer. 'I was there with Marjorie one afternoon,' he said at last. 'It was the spring before she died. I can't tell you what a wonderful few hours we had, what a wonderful sense of peace and love. As though all we'd striven for and failed to achieve during our marriage, had been granted us. The memory of it still comforts me. My only mystical experience, I think. Perhaps the only one I've ever needed.'

His voice faltered, but he quickly recovered himself. 'The birds of Rhiannon,' he said again, in his lecturer's voice, 'What are they? What is magic? Mysticism? Religion? Simply this: something we need in order to bridge the gap between the world we know and understand, and the terrifying darkness of our dreams.'

'I suppose so,' Marian said absently. She knew he was trying to explain something to himself rather than to her, and while he was still deep in thought, she poured herself — and him — another cup of tea.

'Are you visiting Sally later on?' he asked her after a while. 'I'd like to come with you, but I suppose I should stay in tonight.'

'Of course you should. You should go to bed now with your portable television. I'll bring you some supper later on. Stella and John are making lasagna with spinach and cottage cheese, but I'll cook you a chop.'

'The lasagna sounds fine. If you think there'll be enough .'

'Oh, there'll certainly be enough. They only know how to cook for parties. They weigh everything in kilos.'

'Are you feeling more reconciled to Stella now?'

'She's very bright and cheerful and she's certainly going out of her way to be helpful.'

'Do you like her?'

'The only reservation I have is that John has just announced that *he's* having a year off college as well. And I think it would be so much better if he finished his course. Don't you? He says that Stella's not confident enough to manage without him. To me, she seems overflowing with confidence. And to think that John was the one I wasn't worried about!'

'I think I approve of his taking a year off,' Gerald said. 'He's bright enough to pick it all up again whenever he wants to. There are too many people so ruthlessly ambitious that they forget all their other obligations.'

For a time they drank their tea in silence, Marian surprised and disappointed at his reaction.

'I've been thinking a great deal about Marjorie,' he said then, in explanation. 'About how badly I treated her.'

'Oh Gerald, she always seemed devoted to you. And very proud of you. I'm sure she realised that you needed to work very hard and be away a great deal.'

'I hadn't even noticed how ill she was.'

Marian chewed her lip. It was one of the first times he'd spoken to her about Marjorie. 'It doesn't do any good, Gerald,' she said. 'We can't live our lives over again. I feel guilty too, if that's any help to you. Perhaps everyone does. Not many people, I'm sure, behave as well as they'd like to.'

'Not many people behave as badly as I did, ' he said flatly.

'Think of that afternoon on Foel Graig,' Marian said. 'You said that helped you. Think of the good things, the good times.'

She got up and took the tray into the kitchen.

Back in the cottage, she sank into an armchair, too tired even to pick up the newspaper. Paul hadn't been in the shop all day and there'd been a surprising number of customers for a Monday.

As well as that, she'd met Gareth for the first time.

When he'd come into the shop and introduced himself, she'd thought he was looking for Paul. 'No, I've already seen Paul,' he said quietly. 'He's feeling better today. I've just come to ask you to tell your friend how guilty I feel about leaving her when I did. She was kind to me, listening to my problems and trying to advise me what to do.'

'She is kind, but she can be ruthless. No-one blames you.'

'Anyway, I blame myself.'

She'd liked him very much. He seemed sincere and dignified and troubled.

'Thank you for coming to see me,' she'd said. 'I'll give Sally your message. She was very worried last night when I told her that the police had taken you in for questioning.'

'Good-bye, then,' he'd said. 'And thank you for trusting me.'

She'd walked with him to the door of the shop.

'You've decided to stay with your wife, after all?'

163

'Yes.'

That's all he'd wanted to tell her.

'Good Luck,' she'd said, holding out her hand.

She hadn't expected to be so moved by him. She could imagine how Paul must be feeling.

She closed her eyes. She could hear John and Stella having a bath together, and she hoped they'd take a long time over it. The way they groped and grabbed at each other was doing her no good. She still had a visit to the hospital to endure and she'd forgotten to buy flowers. Had all the roses been ruined by the storm, she wondered. Probably.

There was a knock at the front door.

She dragged herself out of the chair, not even bothering to run her fingers through her hair before going to answer it.

She found Alan standing on the door-step.

'Oh, it's you,' she said. 'Please come in, won't you.'

She turned from him, collided with the oak chest which had stood in the hall for twelve years, apologised to it, and ploughed ahead into the sitting room which was suddenly filled with a blinding evening light.

'Do sit down,' she said, her voice catching in her throat.

'What's the matter, Marian? Is there something you have to tell me?' His voice was grave, prepared for the worst.

'Good Lord, no. I'm just surprised to see you, that's all.'

'I rang this morning and John said he thought I should come. I told him to tell you I'd be here about five.'

'He didn't mention it. He must have forgotten. Anyway, it's not important. You mustn't worry about Sally. She's fine.'

'Fine? John told me she'd broken her leg in two places and lost her memory.'

'Yes. When I say she's fine, I mean she's fine apart from that. She's recovering — that's what I mean. Do sit down. How are you?'

'Pleased to have an excuse to see you again so soon.'

'To see me?'

'Marian. Why are you behaving to strangely? You did say I could come down some time. Am I in the way tonight? Just tell me if I am.'

There simply aren't the words to let you know just how happy I am to see you, Marian thought. I should need to faint or burst out into an operatic aria. Why am I so healthy and so unmusical? She said nothing.

'Why are you treating me so distantly?' he asked her. 'After all we are 'good friends', aren't we?'

She started to babble incoherently at that point and he opened the corner cupboard and found the whisky and a glass and poured her a drink.

'Sit down,' he said. 'Is there anything you want to tell me?'

There was. But he was Sally's husband and Sally was ill and needed him.

'Not really,' she said. 'I'd better make a move and get us a meal. Visiting is at seven-thirty.'

'Don't get up. I don't want a meal, I managed to grab some lunch. What's the matter? You want to tell me something about Sally, don't you?'

She looked into his eyes. 'No, but there's something I want to tell you about me,' she said, trying not to tremble.

'OK then, Mum,' John said, throwing open the door. 'We'll be eating in exactly...'

'Alan's here,' Marian said. 'You forgot to tell me he'd phoned.'

'I wrote it on the pad in the hall,' he said, 'I thought you always looked there. You always used to.'

Alan and John shook hands and then Stella came in and was introduced.

'How's Virginia?' John asked. 'Has Mum told you that we've phoned to ask her to come down? I haven't seen her for years. I only hope Tim will show up as well. We often talk about Virginia. Is she still going to be a spy?'

'I suppose she could be anything. She turned out very brainy.'

'So Mum tells us. Funny really, considering what she used to be like. I always had to do her homework when you came over on a Sunday. I can't imagine her being clever.'

Marian threw her eyes to the ceiling.

'What are you reading?' Alan asked Stella.

'English,' she said. 'Only I'm giving up for a while, for rather obvious reasons.'

'Well, we must get on with the supper,' John said, 'or you'll be late at the hospital. We've prepared everything. It's just a matter of throwing it all together, now.'

'You can do it,' Stella said. 'I only get in the way. I'll sit here with my feet up.'

'Do you do the Quick Crossword?' she asked Marian, 'or can I have a go at it?'

Marian passed her the newspaper.

'This is a lovely cottage,' Alan said.

'You can stay here whenever you want to.'

Stella looked up, alerted to something in Marian's voice. 'Hey, on second thoughts, I'd better go and help John,' she said, throwing the paper on the floor and bellying out of the room.

As soon as she'd left them, Alan stood up, drew Marian towards him and kissed her.

'I've fallen in love with you,' she said.

They kissed again.

Everything else would probably prove difficult or impossible Marian thought, but at least confessing that truth had been relatively painless. Why should she try to conceal how she felt? They were mature people and old friends...And he surely knew, anyway. Of course he did.

He said nothing.

'And I hope I'll be able to see you from time to time,' she added, wanting to let him know that her expectations were not impossibly high.

'I love you too,' he said, after a long silence. 'I always have, I suppose.'

What a pleasant meal they'd had, the four of them. Marian couldn't remember, afterwards, what they'd talked about, retaining only the impression that she and Stella had gone half-way towards liking each other. Of course, she wasn't good enough for John; she was selfish, determined on her own way, but all the same there was a sharpness and vigour about her which she couldn't help admiring.

After the meal, she and Alan had driven to the hospital.

She'd begun to feel bitter again, on the journey to Tenby. Once more, Sally seemed to be winning. She'd wanted Alan, and she'd managed to lure him to her side, as she'd always lured Dickie in the past.

She would have liked Alan's assurance that he was making only a duty visit, but he seemed withdrawn and pre-occupied, saying very little.

'I'll let you go in on your own,' she'd said, when they arrived at the hospital. 'I'll join you in about half an hour.'

She wanted him to insist that he needed no time on his own, but he agreed to her suggestion. She went up with him in the lift and showed him Sally's ward.

'Thanks,' he said, pressing her hand. He seemed nervous.

She went down to sit in the reception hall. It was exactly seven-thirty.

I'm behaving like a school-girl, she told herself. He loves me, he's told me so. Why should I expect all his love? He loves Hannah, and of course he loves Sally as well, how could he not, after so many years?

Why shouldn't I suffer? Everybody suffers. Paul is suffering, I know he is. So is Gareth, I'm sure. So is Gareth's wife. God, I didn't know love could be as terrible as this.

She tried to breathe deeply and calmly.

Or is this only jealousy? she asked herself. I suppose it is.

And perhaps it's something I can control in time.

She picked up a magazine and examined a knitting pattern for a baby shawl. She could feel little joy at the prospect of being a grand-mother, but perhaps that would come too.

But how could John have done anything as ill-timed as fall in love, she wondered. He'd never, in the past, put anything before his career, his plans.

Love wasn't everything, she'd wanted to tell him when he was talking about taking a year off his studies.

Love is not all, it is not meat nor drink,
Nor slumber, nor a roof against the rain.

Wasn't it though? Wasn't it more than everything? She thought of Mrs Dainton. She couldn't stop talking about her husband, though he'd been dead for over thirty years. My husband was a dirty rotter, but at least he had red blood in his veins. My husband, my husband.

She thought of Paul. What had John said about his wanting her to join him in something or other? The Mill House at Bryn Tirion. It was a beautiful place. It would certainly give them both something to think about.

She went to the phone booth and dialled his number.

'Yes?' he said, so much hope in his voice that she could hardly bear to disappoint him.

'It's only me,' she said. 'Marian. I'm in the hospital waiting to see Sally. I just rang to say that Gareth called in on me earlier on.'

'Yes,' he said. 'He thought he should thank you.'

'He seemed such a very nice person. That's what I wanted to tell you. I wanted you to know how much I liked him. I wanted you to know that I understand how upset you must be.'

'Yes,' he said again. 'Thanks Marian. Thanks for ringing.'

She put the receiver down, realising that he couldn't say any more without breaking down.

TWENTY

I wanted to tell you about Dickie, but I couldn't,' Sally said, as soon as Marian arrived at her bedside.

Marian bent to kiss her.

Sally had been crying, but in spite of that, she was looking frail and beautiful. When I cry, Marian thought, my face gets pink and blotchy, and even when I'm really ill with 'flu, everyone tells me how well I look.

'Don't think I haven't suffered,' Sally said then. 'Did Alan tell you about the time I had to...'

'I told her everything,' Alan said. He was stroking her arm and looking at her with affection and tenderness.

'I wanted to tell you at the time, but Dickie wouldn't let me. He loved you, you see. Wanted to protect you.'

'Yes,' Marian said. She knew he had loved her and the boys. 'It made it very hard for him, I suppose.'

'I hated you for a long time. Though it wasn't your fault — I knew that. The whole thing was my fault, if anyone's. All the same, I suffered most.' CHILDISHNESS .

'Things just happen,' Marian said.

'Yes. It seemed so unimportant at the beginning. Such a little, trivial, unimportant thing. I would never, never, have started it if I'd known it would get so out of hand.' She fell back on to her bank of pillows.

Alan poured her a drink of the grapefruit juice on her locker. She took it from him and had a long drink.

'Ugh,' she said, shuddering delicately, 'It's like drinking needles. Why can't I have wine?'

'Tomorrow,' he told her.

'They think I'll be able to come out tomorrow or the next day,' she told Marian. 'I had some tests this afternoon. I've had a slight concussion but they say there'll be no permanent damage. Alan says he'll stay until I'm fit to go home and then drive me back in the car. It'll be easier than travelling by train, won't it? With this plaster on my leg? Do you mind putting him up?'

Marian shook her head, not daring to say anything.

'Virginia's coming tomorrow,' she said, after a moment or two. 'I phoned her last night. You'll all have to stay for Gerald's party if he's still planning to have it — I think he is. Has Alan told you about John?'

'No,' Alan said. 'I thought you'd want to.'

Sally turned to Marian again, 'What about John?'

'His girlfriend's six months pregnant and he's giving up his course to be with her.'

Sally squeezed her hand. 'Are you very upset?' she asked.

'Yes.' Marian felt comforted by the pressure on her hand. 'Yes, I am.'

'You shouldn't be,' Alan said. 'She seems a nice kid. Very tough and sensible, I thought.'

'If she's so tough and sensible, why is she letting John muck up his last year?'

'That's right,' Sally said. 'Absolutely. If a girl decides to go ahead and have a baby, she should be prepared to make some sacrifices for it. It's her choice.'

'But perhaps they both decided to go ahead and have it,' Alan said. 'Men have got some rights, surely. Look, if it was Virginia, we'd be pleased if Jess was prepared to do the same as John, wouldn't we?'

'If it was Virginia, I'd rather Jess cleared off and disappeared in smoke,' Sally said. 'What's her name, this very tough and sensible kid? I'm going to have a word with her when I get out of here.'

'Don't be silly,' Alan said.

'I felt like saying something myself,' Marian said, 'but I didn't want to antagonise John. I don't want him to think I'm against her. Well I'm not, not exactly. Oh, she's not too bad, I suppose. At least she's lively. One girl he used to bring home did nothing but sit and arrange her hair all day. She was certainly decorative, but I felt she needed a long silver tail to get away with that.'

'Poor Marian,' Sally said. 'You're quite acerbic in your own way. You try too hard to be calm and civilized about everything.'

'It's just as well she does,' Alan said.

They were all silent for a moment or two.

To Marian's surprise, she suddenly saw Alan getting up to go. 'I'll see you tomorrow, love,' he told Sally, bending to kiss her.

'I'll be waiting for you in the car,' he told Marian. 'Come as soon as the bell goes. She's getting tired.'

'Perhaps I'd better come with you,' Marian said. But Sally was pulling her back.

'Don't do any reading, don't watch television, just rest,' Alan said. 'Just concentrate on getting better.'

With a sinking heart, Marian realised that Sally had asked Alan to leave them alone for the last few minutes. What was coming now, she wondered.

'How is Gareth?' Sally asked.

Was it nothing worse? 'He seems all right. He called on me in the shop, asking me to give you his apologies. He was worried because he'd left you on your own.'

'I liked him so much,' Sally said. 'I suppose you must have heard what happened?'

'Yes.' Try as she might, Marian could think of nothing else to say.

'I wasn't trying to prove anything,' Sally went on. 'I wanted you to know that. I don't like gays, I admit it, but I wasn't trying to harm Paul. It was just something that happened. Because we were in that terrible place in that terrible storm. I don't pretend to understand it. I seem to be hazy about so much of that afternoon.'

'I don't suppose any real harm was done,' Marian said. 'I think Paul blames you for everything, but perhaps that makes it easier for him. I have a feeling, though, that Gareth would probably have stayed with his wife in any case.' Tender-hearted men usually did, she thought. Especially when there were children involved.

The bell for the end of visiting time suddenly clanged through the ward and Marian was as relieved to hear it as everyone else.

'I must go,' she started to say.

But Sally pulled her towards her almost as violently as she had on the mountain. 'I haven't finished yet,' she said. Her cheeks were flushed now, her eyes glittering.

Marian sat down again.

'Dickie,' Sally said, clutching Marian's hands. 'I killed him, Marian. I tried to give him up, but I couldn't. I killed him, Marian. I killed him.'

Marian tried to silence her — in her agitation she was speaking so loudly that anyone in the corridor could have heard her — 'Hush,' she said again and again. 'Do be quiet, love. I'll ring for a nurse. You're getting too worked up. You'll have a relapse.'

But Sally wouldn't let her go, only repeated again, 'I killed him. Why else would he have had that heart-attack? It was my fault. I know it was. For three years, I've had that to live with. I loved him. And I wouldn't let him go. And I killed him.'

'He had a weak heart,' Marian said. 'He'd known about it for years.'

What did a lie matter? Dickie was dead. Sally had loved him, probably more than she'd loved anyone in her life.

'You're lying. You're trying to be kind to me. Don't. I have to face the truth. Don't you see?'

Marian broke away from her and tried to speak calmly. 'He had a congenital heart defect,' she said. 'They discovered it in the post-mortem — a faulty aortal valve. And he probably knew about it. He was a doctor, Sally. He would probably have guessed that there was something wrong with him. Look, I have to go now and you must rest. I'm sure you're right to try to face the truth, but don't make it worse than it is. People of forty-five who are perfectly healthy don't die of worry or remorse — though they might like to.'

'Perhaps not,' Sally said, in an altogether lighter voice. 'Bless you Marian. I do love you.'

Love, love, love, Marian thought savagely as she bent to kiss her and then waved to her from the door.

She went to join Alan in the car park.

'Why don't we stay in a hotel tonight?' he asked her. Virginia will be with us tomorrow and Sally may be out on Wednesday. Let's make the most of tonight. Let's sleep together tonight.'

'I couldn't possibly,' Marian said. 'Not tonight nor any other night.'

'Nonsense,' Alan said, starting up the car. 'Now that I've found you again, you surely can't imagine that I'm going to let you go? If tonight doesn't suit you, that's fine. There'll be plenty of other nights.'

What about Hannah? she wanted to ask. What about Sally, who'll need you now more than ever? She was too miserable to say anything.

'Shall we go as far as the sea?' she said then, 'Just for half an hour? You could turn here.'

'Let's go to Provençe,' Alan said. 'Why don't we? Do you remember the little sandy pinewoods where we used to play hide-and-seek with the children? Do you remember the smell of those picnics? The rosemary that grew everywhere? Wood-smoke and pine needles and Galloises and that strong garlic sausage Dickie liked so much. The wine we drank. Well, we couldn't afford the mineral water, could we? What a beautiful summer that was. That green sundress you had. I've always remembered that dress.'

As he talked, she directed him through little crowded streets, past ice-cream vans, fish and chip shops and amusement arcades, until the surprising splendour of the South Esplanade and the always surprising sea brought him back to the present; she heard his intake of breath.

They were very tired; they'd both had an anxious and largely sleepless night. For a time they sat silently in the car, watching people passing by, holiday people in holiday clothes, going out for a meal or a few drinks or a last stroll, calling to one another, laughing, doing their best to be happy.

'Life is so short,' Alan said. 'I can't believe that love can be wrong.'

'But you're married. And Sally needs you. She wants you to go back to her. You surely can't think that I could...'

'No, I don't think you could be the other woman, if that's what you mean. No.'

'What then?'

'I don't know. But somehow I've stopped being angry with Sally. I've been angry with her for years, I think, haven't been able to talk rationally with her for years. Now I'll be able to. We'll be able to sort something out I'm sure. She seems so much better. Did you notice her eyes tonight? She seems almost normal again. It was like old times. We were joking together, being friendly. What ever happened to her on that mountain?'

'I suppose being in such danger brought her to her senses. It must have been that. Something like that.'

After some minutes, they walked down the steps to the beach.

Everyone had left. The sky was white as a clean bowl. The storms of mid-summer were over. The sea was flat, running up the beach quietly and without fuss like a well-behaved child. The seagulls mewed like kittens.

Marian scooped up some sand and dribbled it through her fingers. Wasn't it what she'd wanted? Sally back to normal with Alan at her side seeming ready to forgive and forget? Surely they would drift back together again? Wouldn't that be best for everyone? Oh, there were no answers, no solutions. Only endless questions, endless problems.

The strangest thing was that since being at the hospital, her frenzy for Alan was almost like a dream she'd managed to wake from. Was it seeing him with Sally? She was still fond of him; yes, she loved him, but it had suddenly become, at least for the moment, an adult, manageable sort of love.

She touched his hand. He looked at her and sighed.

This moment will comfort me, she told herself, when everything else has blown away like dust on the wind. (The little passionate bites, the long famished kisses.)

The sea, wide and eternal, seems an appropriate setting for the end of our affair, she thought. (For God's sake stop it. What affair, for God's sake? That one-night stand? Because that's all it was.)

She glanced at him again. He looked much older than he had in Hannah's little flat. (He wouldn't be going back there. He'd left her a letter, he'd told her, explaining that he wouldn't be going back.) Poor Hannah. But she was young. Or did that make it worse? The large photograph of her hanging in the entrance hall, came alive, she came staggering into the flat with rucksack and guitar, looked about her, saw the letter and... oh, please don't cry.

'Oh, please don't cry,' Alan said.

She flicked away a tear from the corner of her eye. She couldn't tell him she was crying for Hannah. It would sound too patronising for words. And anyway it probably wasn't true. No, she was probably crying for herself. 'Do you wish you were young again?' she asked.

He, too, was playing with the sand. 'Why, do you?'

'No. Not if it meant having to give up the boys and...oh, all my friends. No.'

Her sons and her friends and her work. Her life, she told herself, her life, full of complexity and interest. The prospect of buying the Mill House with Paul was suddenly rather thrilling; an enormous challenge. It was a wonderful old place, huge and dilapidated, but full of potential.

And John and Stella and the baby. How exciting that suddenly seemed. John would surely get his degree eventually, and if he didn't, did it matter so much nowadays, when there were no jobs even for graduates? And Stella was bright enough, she'd give her that. She'd grow to love her perhaps. She'd jolly well have to, wouldn't she?

174

And there was Gerald's party to look forward to; gorgeous food and champagne and the weather likely to hold. And how very suitable that he'd become interested in that nice Miss Morris. (She had a tiny pang as she finally relinquished his lovely, gracious, labour-saving house.)

And Virginia was arriving tomorrow. And Tim, problem child, but so loveable, before the end of the week. (And where might that not lead?) There were so many pages to turn.

'I love you,' Alan said softly.

Yes, she did feel enveloped by a calm and rather melancholy tenderness, which though quite different from the excitement which had connected them in London, was still love perhaps. And perhaps truer and finer and more enduring. Oh stop it, she told herself, for God's sake.

And the evening was perfect, the air clean and sharp. The moon, half an hour ago a colourless disc, a cheap capiz shell, now hung in the sky like a pearl, a jewel of great price.

The sea swirled up to them, nearer and nearer, leaving a lace tracery on the beach as it withdrew. It was time to leave.

As she got to her feet, Marian felt as though she were in a concert hall after an evening of thrilling music, that the echo of it would remain with her all her life.

Oh stop it, she said to herself again. For God's sake.